HUNT-U.S. MARSHAL III

TROUBLE UP NORTH

By

WL COX

Paperback Edition

ISBN-13: 978-1492983095

(Cox Publisihing)

ISBN-10: 1492983098

COX PUBLISHING

Helena, Mt

Chapter 1

Denver Begins To Grow

Over the next several months Denver returned to a peaceful growing city. The payroll for the miners was coming through on a timely basis and except for the occasional bar room fight, a horse theft, some missing cattle and a runaway child things were fairly calm.

Hunt had done some research on the property in the remote valley north of Denver where they had arrested some men responsible for numerous murders and robberies and discovered an Irish immigrant by the name of Hansom O'Dales had filed a claim on the property five years prior and built the cabin.

Hansom O'Dales had disappeared from the face of the earth. Hunt checked with all the stores in Denver; no one remembers seeing him for months. The only thing that made sense to Hunt is that the criminals killed him and took over the cabin. And the only people that would know what happened to Hansom O'Dales were hung.

Hunt checked at the bank; Hansom O'Dales had a small amount of cash in the bank, and the bank manager said he doesn't think he's seen him for at least a year. He took $200 out about a year ago to buy some cattle, the bank manager said as he checked his books, that is the last transaction listed for Hansom O'Dales.

Hunt talked to the land office, and they had a record of 887 acres of land known as Hidden Valley located between two mountain ranges. The land office employee got out a map and pointed out the landmarks of the land claim. "It's a very remote area and nearly impossible to get to," the man said to Hunt, "are you sure you want such a place?"

"Yes," Hunt answered, "that's exactly why I like the property, I don't want visitors."

"OK, there are $84.68 worth of taxes due," the land office employee said. "All we can do is file a land abandonment claim and whoever pays the taxes can claim ownership. The only drawback would be if Mr. O'Dales shows up and claims ownership. If that should happen, you will be out the $84.68 that you paid for the taxes and will be forced to vacate the premises."

"I'll take my chances," Hunt said, "here's the $84.68."

The land office employee listed Huntley Porter, occupation, U.S. Deputy Marshal, as the person whom paid the taxes and therefore has the right to claim ownership of the 887 acres known as Hidden Valley. Hunt received a copy of the map showing the boundaries, and then filed for resources, minerals, lumber and water rights before leaving.

Hunt had the next three days off, and the town was quiet so with U.S. Marshal Dodd's blessing he and Jed rode out to Hidden Valley. It was almost two hours later when Hunt and Jed stopped at the place where the shootout had taken place.

Jed was showing Hunt some game trails to help familiarize him with the layout of the land. They continued traveling the side of Devil's Canyon until they came to a high cliff that ran north for miles.

"According to the map," Jed said as he examined it, "that high point up there on the mountain is the boundary marker on the map."

Hunt looked at the map and answered, "According to the map that point is called Devil's Tower."

"Yes, it makes sense," Jed said, "the lines of the property run down the center of the mountain ranges on both sides of the valley and the north end. This southern end appears to be lined by Devil's Gorge."

"Yes, we must have passed the southeast corner when we rode up the trail, we'll have to look for it when we go back," Hunt said.

"Let's ride along the eastern side as closely as we can, I want to check out the land," Hunt said.

Hunt and Jed traveled almost a half mile when they came to a deep crevice that was fifty yards across at the top and narrowed down to only about twenty feet at the base. The water trickling through the crevice seemed to come through a narrow opening in the rocks Hunt looked up the side of the hill, a sheer rock cliff rose high, and above the cliff the peaks appeared to touch the sky.

Hunt and Jed followed the steep decline along the top edge. Hunt was impressed with what he had seen so far. Millions of trees, water, wildlife, majestic rock formations and the mountains gave it a beautiful, secluded setting.

"It sure is a beautiful place," Jed said as they looked around.

"Yes, it sure is," Hunt answered.

"You know," Jed said as he pointed down onto the valley floor, "if you were to clean out some of those trees you could have a fair sized pasture."

"Yes, I'll make a note of that," Hunt answered as he began walking his horse forward again.

Soon they came to the game trail that led north, down to the valley floor, and as they progressed a whitetail doe, and two fawns ran through the timber. They turned and traveled east along the lower side of the steep bank and looked around as they went.

"Looks like someone's been doing some digging along here," Jed said as they rode.

"Yes," Hunt answered, "I noticed that too."

They eventually came to the creek bed that ran along the base of the rock wall. Hunt and Jed dismounted and allowed the horses to drink and graze as they looked around.

"There's a pick and shovel here," Hunt said as he picked them up. Hunt peered into what looked like a cave, actually it was only a hollowed out crevice between the rocks and daylight could be seen on the other side.

"That must be the place we saw from up above, this is the crevice that the water runs through," Hunt said.

"Why would anyone be digging in this rocky ground?" Jed asked.

"I'm not sure," Hunt said, "but maybe he wasn't digging."

"What would the digging tools be for?" Jed asked.

"Could be the old man was looking for gold," Hunt answered.

"No," Jed answered, "the Gold is on the far side of the mountain; that's where the Denver Mine is located about five miles the way the crow flies."

"You're probably right," Hunt said, "but it doesn't stop people from looking for it. Let's go through the crevice and see what's on the other side," Hunt said as he led the way.

After a short walk in the shallow stream they emerged into a serene place isolated from the rest of the world. It was only about a thousand square foot spot surrounded by rock and the stream water disappeared into a narrow crack in the rock wall.

"I'll bet in the spring when the stream is running high water fills this section," Jed said as he examined the water stains on the stone walls.

"Yes, that's probably why the rocks are so smooth," Hunt answered.

"Hey," Jed said, "look over in the corner, that looks like a boot sticking out of the ground."

They walked over and pulled on the boot, but it seemed to be attached.

"Go get the shovel," Hunt said, "I think we just found Hansom O'Dales."

A short time later they found the remains of an old man buried in a shallow grave covered with sand and silt.

His coat was riddled with bullet holes, and there was a bullet hole in his head. Jed went back to the horses and retrieved a blanket, and they wrapped the body. They carried the body out and laid it on the grassy slope by the stream.

"He's not going anywhere," Hunt said, "and those that killed him are dead, so let's continue on and we'll pick him up on the way back."

They spent most of the day riding around the side of the property. Game was plentiful, and they found a small waterfall at the north end of the valley.

Then at the northwest corner they found a narrow valley leading through the mountain. They decided to follow it and found that it led out of the valley onto the forest floor. They continued traveling and came to the old trail that would take them back to Denver.

"What are the chances of finding this entrance again from outside?" Jed asked, "trees are every-where, and the terrain looks the same for miles."

"Well," Hunt said as he dismounted, "I have an idea."

Hunt walked up to the large tree that was near the road and carved the initials, NW, onto it.

11

"This will indicate the northwest entrance," Hunt said, "and we'll be the only two that know about it, for a while anyway."

"Well now, let's see if we can find our way back," Jed said as he laughed, turned his horse and followed Hunt back the way they had come. They found the opening through the mountain and Hunt stopped.

"This must be how old man O'Dales got his wagon to the cabin," Hunt said.

"Yes," Jed answered, "it makes sense. He'd have one hell of a time trying to get it down that game trail from the south."

"I wonder what other secrets he knew about," Hunt said.

"I'm sure whatever they are you'll figure them out," Jed said with a chuckle.

They rode to the cabin and dismounted.

"I think," Hunt said, "it will be easier to take the old man's body back to town in the wagon."

"My horse has never pulled a wagon," Jed said.

"Mine either," Hunt answered, "but we can put our saddles in the wagon. Let's go inside and look around."

Hunt made a note of everything inside the cabin. Some homemade furniture, a bed, a cast iron pot and pan, a tin plate, a few tin cups, a table, two chairs, a cook stove and a fireplace with a cast iron poker.

"It sure isn't much of a place," Jed said as they looked around.

"No, but it's a start," Hunt answered, "it's got everything a man needs."

"There's no food, just a bunch of empty cans. The gang that was staying here must have helped themselves," Hunt said.

"It don't look like he was much of a brick mason either," Jed said, "that rock looks loose."

Hunt pulled the rock, and it lifted out of its place. Inside it was hollow, Hunt looked in the hole and there was a small bag. He pulled it out and looked inside then poured the contents into his hand.

"Gold!" Jed said as his eyes bulged, "there must be close to an ounce!"

"Yes," Hunt answered, "there should be enough here to buy a plot in the cemetery, a headstone, and pay the mortician."

"Hunt," Jed said with worried tone, "when we get back to town double check with the land office and make sure you have the mineral, water, and precious metals rights to the land."

13

"Yes, minerals, precious metals, water, and lumber too," Hunt added. "I applied for the lumber, water, and minerals, but I didn't think about the precious metals."

"Let's hitch up the horses to the wagon," Hunt said, "we've got a body to haul into town."

Hunt and Jed unsaddled the horses and soon had them hitched to the wagon with the harness they found in the shack used as a shelter for the horses. Then they placed their saddles into the wagon. The horses weren't used to pulling a wagon, and it took them a little while but eventually they got the hang of it.

Hunt and Jed picked up Hansom O'Dales body and laid him in the wagon, then they drove the wagon out the narrow canyon and turned south on the old trail leading to Denver.

It was 5:00 in the afternoon when they reached Denver and Hunt stopped in front of the U.S. Marshal Office. Hunt went in and told U.S. Marshal Dodd what they found, and he came out to examine the body.

"It's hard to tell," Dodd said, "the body is pretty badly decomposed but judging by where you found him I'd venture to bet it's Hansom O'Dales."

Hunt and Jed rode to the mortuary and parked the wagon in the back. They knocked on the door, and it was opened. Hunt filled the mortician in on what was going on, and the mortician had him, and Jed bring the body in and laid him on a table.

"Do what you have to do," Hunt said, "I want him buried in the cemetery. Pick him out a nice pine box and bury him tomorrow."

Hunt heard the back door open, and Clayton walked in.

"Deputy," Hunt said, "what brings you around this evening?"

"Just making my rounds," Clayton answered, "I saw the wagon and heard voices, and I just thought I'd check it out."

Hunt explained to Clayton about finding the body and bringing it in.

Clayton looked at the body and shook his head. "He's got five bullet holes in his jacket, and one in his head; looks like someone emptied their gun into him."

"Yes," Hunt answered, "or there was more than one man shooting."

"It's too bad," Clayton said as he looked at the body, "does he have any kin?"

"Not around here," Hunt answered. "The land office agent told me he came from Ireland; he may have kinfolk in Ireland, but not here. I plan to try to get an address in Ireland and send off a

15

letter, the kinfolk in Ireland have a right to know what happened to him and that we hung those responsible for his death."

Chapter 2

Trouble In The Far North

A week passed since Hansom O'Dales was buried. Hunt found an address in Dublin, Ireland and wrote to the family and told them of Hansom's demise and how the people responsible were shot, and the rest of them were hung. Then Hunt included a copy of the newspaper article regarding the trial and the hanging in the letter.

Hunt spent a few days out in Hidden Valley after making sure all mineral and precious metals rights remained in his name.

"Evidence of finding precious metals must be displayed within one year from the date of filing, otherwise, anyone that finds precious metals has the right to file a mining claim," the land office agent said as he peered over his wire rim glasses.

Hunt removed the small black bag and sat it on his desk, "is this proof enough?" He asked.

The Land Agent was ecstatic, "where did you find this?" He asked.

"On my property," Hunt answered. "And if I find anyone on my property looking for Gold they'll be shot," so keep your mouth shut.

So the Land Agent completed the paperwork necessary to certify the claim of all precious metals on the land in Hunt's name.

Hunt sold the 1.3 ounces of Gold and received $56.78. Hunt went to the undertakers and paid for the burial plot and the mortician's services. Hunt had $32 left; he added $18 for the wagon and three head of cattle Hunt found on the property and included the $50 with a letter to Hansom O'Dales kinfolk in Ireland.

"You went to a lot of troubles bringing his body in for burial," Earl said, "why don't you just keep the $32 for services rendered?"

"Somebody in Ireland is going to be mighty sad when they get my letter," Hunt answered, and the $50 will at least be giving them something that they will remember him for. It may provide them some cash to have a wake in his memory, or maybe buy some groceries."

"Either that or they'll be at the pub getting drunk on your money," Earl said.

"It's not my money," Hunt reminded him, "it belongs to Hansom O'Dales."

Hunt and Earl walked to the U.S. Marshal office.

"Hunt," U.S. Marshal Dodd said as they walked in. "I need to talk to you."

"I received an official letter from Washington," Dodd said. "There are two army scouts missing. According to the letter these scouts are the scum of the earth. Claims of rape, murder and robbery have been filed against them."

"The problem is they have disappeared from the face of the earth. Some speculate they traveled west to Oregon or California. Others speculate Indians killed them. Of course they could have traveled back east, or gone to Canada," Dodd added.

"If they ran away from their duties they are wanted for desertion. And if Indians killed them then we need to know by whom and why they were killed," Dodd said as he looked up at the three men standing at his desk.

"If they were found," Hunt asked, "wouldn't they just be hung?"

"Yes, they probably would be, but the government wants to know what happened to them, they don't take desertion lightly," Dodd said.

"Earl, I want you go with him," Dodd said as he looked at Earl.

"What about me?" Jed asked.

"No," Dodd answered, "I need you here. With Hunt gone, I'll make you second in command until Hunt returns."

"Hunt," U.S. Marshal Dodd said, "this kind of a journey requires a man that can live off the land, survive and come back in one piece. With your experience and background in tracking and living off the land, I think you're the best one to send."

"Here's an old map," U.S. Marshal Dodd said as he opened a folded map and spread it out on the table. "The scouts were assigned to Ft. Carson up here in the Dakota and Montana territory. You'll be traveling through Indian territory so be careful. Any questions?"

"How long do you think the trip will take?" Hunt asked.

"If I haven't heard from you in six weeks I'll get worried," Dodd answered. "I want each of you to take two extra boxes of ammo and take two canteens each. Be sure to take a knife, a pistol and a rifle. Have a safe trip, try to stay in touch and I'll see you soon I hope."

Hunt and Earl went to their hotel rooms and checked out with their gear, saddled their horses and rode to the general store where Hunt purchased two dozen cigars. As they passed the Sheriff's office, they saw Clayton walking the sidewalk. Hunt stopped and told him where they were headed, Clayton wished them well, and they rode off.

It was late afternoon when they left Denver, several hours later they passed the mountain range where Hunt's Hidden Valley property lay.

"I have an idea," Hunt said to Earl, "how would you like to sleep under a roof tonight instead of out on the prairie?"

"Sounds good to me," Earl answered.

"Follow me," Hunt said as he turned at the tree marked with the NW.

"See the mark on that tree?" Hunt asked.

"Yes," Earl answered, "what does NW mean?"

"This is the trail leading to the northwest corner of my property," Hunt answered. "Remember the trail we take, it may save your life someday. Jed and I found it one day when we were checking the terrain around my property."

Earl followed Hunt as he led him through the forest, half way there Hunt stopped and pointed to a large rock protruding up from the top of the mountain.

"If you ever get lost, ride towards that rock," Hunt said as he pointed.

Hunt continued on and soon they came to the narrow entrance and traveled through the canyon in the shallow stream. A short time later they stopped at the corral and they removed the saddles and put the horses in the corral. Hunt set out some hay from the barn as the horses drank from the shallow stream flowing through the corral.

Hunt and Earl carried their saddlebags and rifles into the cabin. They built a fire in the fireplace and ate. They slept well and were up before daylight, saddled their horses and were miles away from the cabin when the sun came up. Hunt liked traveling with Earl, and Earl felt comfortable in Hunt's company. They made a good pair.

The horses were in top shape. They covered nearly forty miles by noon when they stopped at a stream to rest the horses and allow them to drink and graze while they ate in a grassy cove.

After a forty-five-minute rest, they tightened the cinches on the saddles, mounted and progressed on their journey. It was 5:00

in the afternoon when they stopped to water the horses and let them rest. As Hunt and Earl ate, Hunt took out the map.

"We're near the town of Greeley, Hunt said, "With a little luck we could spend the night in a hotel and restock our food supply."

"Sounds good," Earl answered, "let's get moving."

They were soon mounted and walking their horses at a good pace. Earl's horse was sound and long legged, and it was able to match Hunt's horse's pace. Because Hunt didn't have to hold his horse back they made good time.

It was growing dark when they arrived in Greeley, which wasn't much of a town. They spent the night in a boarding house and stabled their horses in the barn that belonged to the owners. They spent a good night, got a good meal of steak, potatoes and beans and sat on the front porch with the owners and smoked a cigar.

Hunt told them they would be leaving before daylight, so the Mrs. of the house told them she would get up early and fix them breakfast.

After eating breakfast, they remembered they needed a few supplies, so they waited for the general store to open and stocked up on supplies and then rode out of town. The town of Cheyenne, Wyoming, was a good day's ride. They were told it wasn't much of a town, however, they would be able to get a place to sleep and a cooked meal.

After leaving Cheyenne they traveled north looking for the mountain range and spent the next two nights sleeping under the stars. On the third day after leaving Cheyenne they came upon an Indian village.

The Indian scouts spotted them and rode up to them. Hunt sat on his horse and waited as they approached.

"Earl," Hunt said, "act normally, don't show fear."

Five warriors rode up to them and spoke in their native language.

Hunt couldn't understand what they were saying and then one of the braves motioned for them to follow him. He led them down to the central camp littered with close to a hundred teepees.

A warrior approached, "I am Smoking Cloud," he said in English.

Hunt was relieved that he understood English. "My name is Hunt," he said, "and this is Earl."

"What tribe is this?" Hunt asked.

"We are Cheyenne," Smoking Cloud answered. Why does the white lawman travel this far north?" He asked.

"We're on our way to Fort Carson," Hunt answered. "Do you know where the fort is located?"

The warrior explained to them by drawing a map in the dirt with a stick.

"Beware," Smoking Cloud cautioned them, "avoid the western pass and the Blackfeet."

Smoking Cloud drew a crude map in the dirt and showed him the boundaries of the land that lay ahead and what to avoid.

"Smoking Cloud," Hunt said, "have you ever seen the white scouts from the fort?"

Hunt described them and told Smoking Cloud that he was looking for them to take back to the white man's court to stand trial for crimes.

"Yes," Smoking Cloud answered, "I remember two white men came to trade and then they asked about a white man they were looking for. They became angry when we told them we didn't know him, but the Sioux said they found the bones of a man and a pair of sandals near the Blackfoot River. We told them the Sioux buried the bones."

"After they became angry our chief ordered them to leave. The large man with a scar on his face told me that if he finds out we're hiding this man that he would lead the soldiers here and kill everyone in the camp," Smoking Cloud said.

"How long ago was this?" Hunt asked Smoking Cloud.

"One summer ago," Smoking Cloud answered.

"Have you seen the two white men since that day?" Hunt asked.

"No, we have not," he answered.

"Have you heard any stories from other tribes about these white men?" Hunt asked.

"It is said," Smoking Cloud said to Hunt and Earl, "that the two men went to the Sioux camp and there was trouble. The Sioux said the white men were ordered to leave. They left the camp and traveled west towards the Blackfeet land. No one has heard from them since that day," he answered.

"Who is the white man that they were looking for?" Hunt asked.

"They said it was a man that had traveled from the Far East; he was a killer and there was a reward of many dollars on his head," Smoking Cloud answered.

"Have you heard of any new people coming through within the past two years?" Hunt asked.

"There is only one, he is living with the Sioux. They say he has strong medicine; he has killed many in combat. Many speak of him over campfires; they talk of his great medicine. Enemies fear him, and they tell many stories about him," Smoking Cloud answered.

"Have you ever met him?" Hunt asked.

"Yes, we were asked to help the Sioux when the Pawnee and Shoshone attacked wagons from the fort that were traveling to the Sioux camp to build a school. Many died that day; it was a great battle. That is the day I met Storm Warrior. He fought bravely and killed many," Smoking Cloud answered.

"Who is Storm Warrior?" Hunt asked.

"The warrior with green eyes that joined the Sioux," he answered.

Hunt remembered the man he tracked across the plains was said to have green eyes, could it be the same man? He wondered.

"Why do they call him Storm Warrior?' Hunt asked.

"It is said he was traveling with a small Sioux war party. The Pawnee had attacked the Sioux camp and had stolen ponies. Chief Gray Horse took a small war party to search for the ones that had attacked their camp," Smoking Cloud explained.

"One of the Pawnee had stolen Gray Horse's war pony. They found the Pawnee that had raided the Sioux camp and Gray Horse killed the warrior that was riding his pony," he added.

27

"They were returning to the Sioux camp when they found a strangely dressed man riding a mare. They thought he was Pawnee and surrounded him. It is said a young warrior walked up to him to cut his throat, but Storm Warrior broke his arm. Then Storm Warrior patched his arm, with sticks and leather thongs," Smoking Cloud said.

"Chief Gray Horse allowed him to live, and he traveled with the Sioux," Smoking Cloud continued. "That night they made camp and were attacked by a Pawnee war party. It is said Storm Warrior fought bravely and killed many enemy. During the battle he saved the one with the broken arm."

"The next day they traveled across the prairie and camped in the Valley of Tears. That night Storm Warrior went to a small hill and prayed while the Sioux watched. A large war party of Pawnee was traveling to get ahead of the Sioux and cut them off," he said.

"After Storm Warrior prayed a great storm came. The Sioux took shelter under a large overhang of stone against the valley floor, but the Pawnee was on open ground. The great storm killed many Pawnee; the wind blew weapons away and scattered the ponies," Smoking Cloud added.

"After the storm the Pawnee were left with no ponies and no weapons. Many were gone, carried away by the strong winds.

From that day on the Sioux called him Storm Warrior," Smoking Cloud explained.

"That is a very interesting story," Hunt said.

"They say when he prays his God speaks to him and tells him what to do," Smoking Cloud continued, "the stories around campfires say that no warrior can defeat him. He has set up a training camp and teaches the young braves how to fight. The Sioux have made him a Chief. He is much respected by the Sioux and feared by the enemy."

"Earlier you spoke of wagons going to the Sioux camp to build a school," Hunt said, "Who will teach at this school?"

"A white woman with yellow hair from the wagon train will teach English words to the Sioux. It is said she is Storm Warrior's squaw," he answered.

"Smoking Cloud," Hunt said, "we need to travel to the fort and should be going."

Hunt and Earl thanked Smoking Cloud for his hospitality, mounted their horses and rode north.

As they rode, Hunt and Earl talked about the Sioux called Storm Warrior.

"I think," Hunt said, "he is the one I had tracked from Boston to the Missouri River. There was a $1000 bounty on his head for killing someone on the ship and escaping."

"It could be," Earl answered, "the two missing white scouts found him and tried to take him for the reward and either the Sioux killed them or Storm Warrior killed them."

"At this point," Hunt said, "I'm convinced they're dead."

"Yes, you are probably right," Earl said. "If they were alive we'd be hearing stories of rape, murder and robbery. No one can find any sign of them after visiting the Sioux camp."

They had traveled ten miles since leaving the Cheyenne camp and found a secluded spot at the foot of a mountain with a spring.

"We'll make camp and get some sleep," Hunt said to Earl.

Early the next morning they ate a quick breakfast and were mounted and traveling as the sun rose. They rode the horses at a fast walk and by noon they had arrived at the pass that Smoking Cloud had warned them about.

Hunt looked at the map and made changes in the terrain where the Blackfoot River was drawn on the map.

"That must be the pass," Hunt said as he pointed towards the opening in the mountains, "where the wagon train was wiped out that Smoking Cloud spoke of."

"According to Smoking Cloud we should turn right," Hunt said.

"Hey," Earl said, "we're being watched."

A lone Indian sat on a horse watching them.

"Let's be friendly and ride up to him," Hunt said, "leave your rifle in the scabbard but be sure you can get to your pistol fast if you need to."

They walked their horses towards the waiting Indian. As they approached and stopped Hunt raised his hand, "hello," Hunt said.

The Indian just looked at them but didn't speak.

"Do you speak English?" Hunt asked him.

"You wear a shining star of the white man's law," he said.

Hunt and Earl were surprised that he could speak English. "We are U.S. Deputy Marshals," Hunt answered.

"Why are U.S. Marshals on Blackfeet land?" He asked.

"I was told this is Cherokee land," Hunt answered as he stared back harshly. "The land that lies beyond the river is Blackfeet land."

"My name is Hunt," Hunt said as he continued, "and this is Earl, what is your name?"

"I am Bull," he answered as he pounded his chest with his fist, "I am a Blackfeet warrior."

Hunt didn't smile; he just stared back and said, "Nice to meet you Bull."

"We are looking for two white men that worked for the fort as scouts, they have been missing for almost a year. Do you know anything about them?" Hunt asked.

"The winds say there were two white men trading with the tribes, the winds say they were bad medicine, and it is said the Sioux killed them," Bull answered. "It is said their bones litter the ground of a box canyon on Sioux land. There is a spring in the canyon. The white men were filled with bad medicine, now the Blackfeet calls the springs Bad Medicine Springs. The canyon is evil, many Blackfeet have died there."

'Have you ever seen these white men?" Hunt asked.

"Yes, one summer ago they came to our village to trade. They had poisoned tongues and evil spirits filled their bodies. We did not like them and ordered them to leave, and they became angry," Bull answered.

"Before they left they asked about a white man with green eyes, they say he was last seen after crossing the great river to the east that the white man calls Missouri. We told them we knew nothing of such a man. They became angry and said we knew whom they were talking about. Our warriors surrounded them with rifles and we ordered them to leave or die, so they left," Bull answered.

"This man with green eyes, have you ever seen him or know of him?" Hunt asked.

"I know of no white man with green eyes," Bull answered. "Green eyes are rare, but it is said there is a mighty Sioux warrior named Storm Warrior, they say his eyes are green. They say his medicine is powerful; it is said no man can defeat him in battle, and he has killed many."

"Have you ever seen this warrior named Storm Warrior?" Hunt asked.

"Only from a great distance," Bull answered, "I would have challenged him, but he was traveling with over three thousand Sioux. There was a large white man; they rode their ponies to the bottom of a hill at the foot of a mountain that the Sioux calls Bear Mountain."

"I was in the rocks high on the mountain and watched to see what they were doing. Storm Warrior and the white man fought with knives. Storm Warrior defeated him; the white man was on the ground and could not get up, but he was not yet dead," Bull said as he continued.

"Then a large bear came from the forest below me and challenged Storm Warrior. The bear stood on its back legs and growled loudly at Storm Warrior. I thought I would see the bear kill Storm Warrior. Storm Warrior only came to the bear's chest when the bear stood up and pawed the air and roared," Bull said.

"Storm Warrior stood before the bear and did not move," Bull said as his eyes changed, "Storm Warriors eyes glowed with fire, his hair was white and his body seemed to glow, it was as if his body was burning on the inside."

"The bear dropped down on all four legs, and picked up the white man and carried him to the forest. The white man was screaming; the bear dropped him, picked him up by the head and shook him. I heard the neck break and then the bear picked him up and carried him into the forest and up the mountain," Bull added.

"Then the Sioux shouted war hoops. A young brave brought Storm Warrior's horse to him, and he rode up the hill to the waiting chiefs. There was a wagon with a white woman, she had yellow hair, and two white scouts were with the Sioux," Bull said.

"Are you sure he was Storm Warrior?" Hunt asked.

"At first I was not sure," Bull said, "Storm Warrior's hair was white, but he moved and fought like Storm Warrior. There is no other that can fight as he fights. His medicine is strong. The white man was much larger, but Storm Warrior stabbed him with his knife and kicked him in the leg breaking his knee."

"When Storm Warrior fights he is quick, and ferocious as a bear. So far all that have challenged him have died, and it is said he has never been scratched," Bull said.

"Do you think you could defeat him?" Hunt asked.

"Only I could defeat him," Bull said, "but if I die then I will know that I died by the best warrior. And if I defeat him I will take his scalp for all to see and ride his black stallion that so many want."

"We are headed for the fort Bull, thank you for the information. Your men are waiting for you," Hunt said as he pointed up the mountain to a group of six warriors sitting on horseback a half mile away.

"Bull turned and looked to see what Hunt was pointing at, "they are Blackfeet warriors posted to guard the pass, I am not riding with them, but I will tell them why you are here and to enable you to pass on to the fort in peace, they will not attack you."

"Thank you Bull," Hunt said, "I hope we meet again someday."

Bull just looked at him and didn't answer. Bull watched as they turned their horses and rode away. He noticed they had their pistols exposed and easy to pull from their holsters. With two of them he had little chance, but he liked the looks of the horse that the one called Hunt rode. He watched as they rode away then turned his pony and galloped towards the waiting warriors.

"Who are they?" One of the waiting warriors asked as Bull approached.

"They wear a tin star and say they are U.S. Marshals," Bull answered.

"Why are they here?" He asked.

"They are looking for the two white traders that were in our camp last summer," Bull answered.

"The ones filled with bad medicine?" The scout asked.

"Yes," Bull answered.

"Did you tell them the Sioux killed them?" He asked.

"Yes," Bull answered, "I told them that the words in the wind say the Sioux killed them."

"That is good," the scout said as Bull rode away.

Hunt and Earl traveled over a mile and looked behind them and no one was following much to the relief of Earl. Both horses walked briskly, and they covered ground quickly as they kept the horses moving.

"What do you think about the Indian we met?" Earl asked.

"I think," Hunt answered, "that if one of us were alone he would have tried to kill to take the guns, horse, and supplies."

"Yes," Earl answered, "he doesn't appear to be a real friendly kind of guy."

"Do you think this Storm Warrior guy is the same one that you trailed all across the west?" Earl asked.

"I don't know," Hunt answered, "but how many men do you know with green eyes?"

"Yes," Earl answered, "especially an Indian."

Hunt and Earl continued riding while keeping an eye on possible ambush places as they traveled.

They had traveled almost thirty miles since meeting Bull at the mouth of the pass. They stopped at the site of the Blackfeet attack against the wagon train that had occurred months earlier. There were graves near the foot of the mountain, and they rode over to investigate the markers.

"The graves don't look old Hunt," Earl said as they sat on their horses and looked at the long row of graves.

"No, they don't," Hunt answered. "Judging by the grass and weeds growing on the dirt I'd say they were probably buried last spring."

Hunt and Earl rode up and down the row of graves looking at the names on the markers.

Some were names of soldiers and others had Indian names.

"It's strange to have soldiers and Indians buried side by side," Earl said.

Unknown to Hunt and Earl Sioux scouts had been watching them for hours as they traveled east along the river towards the fort.

"Look over there," Earl said as he pointed to the north.

Hunt looked to where he was pointing, "smoke signals," Hunt answered.

"They're probably telling someone about us," Hunt said.

"Isn't that Sioux land?" Earl asked.

"It is according to my map," Hunt answered as he noted the site of the graves on the map . "I think we should keep moving;

this could be some sort of sacred ground to them, and all these graves give me the jitters."

Hunt and Earl once again walked their horses as they chewed on jerky. Both Hunt and Earl kept an eye on the landscape but never saw a single person and yet from time to time they saw smoke signals as they kept moving.

At nightfall, they came to a well-used campsite. Remains of old campfires were evident. Hunt rode his horse to the riverbank, and old wagon wheel marks showed that wagons had crossed here in the past. Ahead lay a trail that had old wagon wheel marks in the trail. Hunt and Earl rode their horses around and investigated the area.

"Looks like this is as good of a place to camp as any," Hunt said as he looked around.

"What do you make of this place?" Earl asked.

"Looks like wagons from the fort camped here and then crossed the river," Hunt answered.

"I'll bet if you were to follow those wagon tracks north it would lead to the Sioux camp. And if you were to follow those in the morning going east I'd say it would lead to the fort. Let's camp here in the cove, we'll water the horses, and then tie them back here in the cove," Hunt said as he dismounted.

Firewood was plentiful; they built a small fire and cooked up rabbits they had shot earlier. The horses grazed on the tall grass as Hunt and Earl slept. Coyotes were calling higher on the mountain behind them, and Hunt didn't sleep well. The sun was just starting to rise as Hunt heated up some coffee and soon they were mounted and riding east following the trail to the fort.

The trail took them through the forest and then it opened out into rolling hills. Finally, they came to the forest once again and after passing through the forest they came out into the opening again with the fort in sight a half mile away.

As they continued riding they heard a bugle sounding the alert of riders approaching. Hunt noticed the cabins close to the fort with a small crowd of men collected around a fire pit holding rifles. Several men came to the gate of the fort as they approached and they halted the horses at the gate.

"Who are you?" A sergeant asked.

"We're U.S. Deputy Marshals out of Denver," Hunt answered. "I need to see your commanding officer."

"What about?" The sergeant asked.

"That Sergeant," Hunt answered, "is none of your business."

"Just then a man approached with Captain bars on his uniform.

40

"Stand down Sergeant," the Captain ordered.

"What can I do for you gentlemen?" The Captain asked.

"We're U.S. Deputy Marshals from Denver," Hunt answered, "we need to speak with your commanding officer."

"Of course," the Captain answered, "come this way."

"Sergeant," the Captain said, "Take their horses to the stable and make sure they have food and water."

Hunt and Earl followed the Captain to the stairs and climbed to enter the Colonel's office.

"Sir," Captain Blanchard announced, "these men are U.S. Deputy Marshals from Denver. They've asked to speak to you."

Hunt and Earl removed their coats and their U.S. Marshal badges pinned to their shirts became visible.

"Of course gentlemen, I am Lt. Colonel Hawks, have a seat," the Lt. Colonel said as they shook hands. "Captain," the Lt. Colonel said; "join us please."

All four sat at a table; introductions were made. Hunt told him they were sent to investigate the disappearance of the two scouts hired by the government. "Do you have any idea what could have happened to them?" Hunt asked.

41

"I wished I knew the answer to that one," Lt. Colonel Hawks answered. "They left on a scouting mission one day and never returned. And actually, when they returned I was going to have them arrested. We got word that they have been involved in criminal activity involving some settlers. They were a mean pair, and I can't believe the government hired them."

"Yesterday morning Earl and I met a Blackfoot by the name of Bull. Do you know him?" Hunt asked.

"No, I don't know him," Lt. Colonel Hawks answered.

"He speaks English, but he didn't seem to be real friendly," Hunt said.

"He claims," Hunt continued, "last year, two men matching their description came to visit their camp. He also said that they were asking about a white man with green eyes that they believed to have traveled this way. Bull said when they told the men they didn't know anything about him and the two became rude and angry. Then some warriors with rifles surrounded them and made them leave. He says that's the last time he ever seen them."

"It sounds like those two," the Colonel answered. "They were nothing but trouble. They carried a wanted poster for a man last seen headed this way. There was a thousand dollar bounty on his head. I told them that the poster was worthless. A ship captain posted the reward, and when the ship left port it disappeared. Even

42

if someone did find him, and brought him back there is no one to pay the reward. It would all be for nothing," the Colonel added.

"Yes," Hunt answered, "I heard the same story about the ship Captain. Before I was a U.S. Deputy Marshal, I worked as a bounty hunter. I tracked the man all the way to the Missouri river."

"Along the way," Hunt said as he continued, "I picked up another criminal.The man I was tracking had run into the criminal I arrested and his partner one day, and they tried to rob him of a fancy knife that he carried."

"The one I was tracking killed one guy by swiping his knife across his throat and kicked the other man in the chest so hard that I think it cracked his chest bone," Hunt said as he continued. "They had two horses, one was turned loose and he mounted the other and traveled west."

"I was making good time tracking him but after he acquired the horse I wasn't able to catch up to him before he crossed the Missouri River. With winter coming on and a prisoner in tow, I had no choice. I returned to Indiana with the prisoner, and the prisoner I brought back was hung," Hunt explained.

"It's a long story," Hunt said, "but along the way I met a U.S. Marshal that rode with me and after the trial he offered me a job with the U.S. Marshals, I accepted and here I am."

"So you are no longer looking for this man?" The Colonel asked.

"No, not really, but I would like to know what happened to him and maybe even sit down and have a drink with him. People I met along the trail that did meet him all liked him. They say he was polite, worked for a meal, and even prayed. Not one person had a bad word to say about him, except for the guy he kicked in the chest, that is," Hunt said with a smile.

"The Colonel chuckled, "yes, I don't suppose he would have much good to say."

"I was told," Hunt continued, "that there is a Sioux by the name of Storm Warrior that has green eyes, do you know this man?"

"Yes," the Colonel answered, "I know him."

"I think," Hunt added, "he could be the man that I tracked all the way to the Missouri River."

"It could be," the Colonel answered, "but I'll tell you this. If it is him keep quiet about it. If you try to arrest him or take him away thousands of Sioux will be after your scalp. Storm Warrior is a Chief and a few weeks before you arrived, he married a widow from a wagon train massacre."

"My soldiers built a schoolhouse with living quarters at one end but the Sioux would not allow a single woman to live among them, so she married Storm Warrior. She's a school-teacher and will teach English to the children. It is Storm Warrior's plan to educate the Sioux," Lt. Colonel Hawks said.

"Storm Warrior saved my life," the Captain added. "The wagons were circled; the soldiers emptied their guns, and the Blackfeet kept coming. Soon everyone inside the wagon circle was in hand-to-hand combat, and the Blackfeet was winning. All of a sudden Storm Warrior rode his horse between the wagons and leaped on an Indian that had one of the soldiers down and about to split his skull with a hatchet."

"He started killing Blackfeet with his knife; I was pinned against a wagon wheel with an arrow in my shoulder and Storm Warrior came to my rescue, more Blackfeet attacked and he easily handled them. The next thing we knew more Sioux stormed into the wagon circle and then it was over. The Sioux are ferocious in battle and take no prisoners. I was wounded and was moments away from being killed when Storm Warrior came between the charging Blackfeet and me. I owe him my life," Captain Blanchard said.

"Out of gratitude, I gave Storm Warrior a parade uniform saber," the Captain said as he continued "But he said he could only take it if I allowed him to give me something in return. I said it wasn't necessary, but he insisted or he wouldn't accept the saber; so I agreed."

"Storm Warrior rides a magnificent black stallion that he calls Wind Fire. He is giving me one of its colts after it is weaned. The Lieutenant has seen it, and he claims it is the pride of the herd," Captain Blanchard said with a smile.

"From the way you speak of this Storm Warrior you make him out to be a hero," Hunt said.

"He's more than that," the Colonel added, "He is a legend. The other tribes all fear him, many challenged him, and all have died."

"Even our infamous Sargent Black challenged him one day here at the fort," the Colonel added. "Sargent Black fancies himself a fighter, he brags of being a boxing champion back east. So he and Storm Warrior squared off outside in a friendly match. A few minutes later Sargent Black was thrown against a hitching post so hard that it broke off at the ground and he couldn't get up."

"I was upset with him for challenging Storm Warrior, so I made him repair the broken hitching post and then stand guard till midnight," Lt. Colonel Hawks added.

"So," Hunt asked, "did he ever hit Storm Warrior?"

"Not once," the Colonel answered.

"I think," the Colonel added, "you are one lucky man that you didn't catch up to him before he crossed the Missouri."

"And why is that?" Hunt asked.

The Colonel sat back in his chair and looked at him, "until you see him in action you'll never be able to understand what I'm saying. He is a one-man army, and you never want to fight him one on one, if you try, you will lose."

"Storm Warrior is indeed a legend and a great man. If and when you finally meet him, treat him with respect," the Colonel warned Hunt, "all that have met him like him, I certainly do, and he is a good man, and any man that tries to do him harm will have to deal with the entire Sioux nation. And that is a hornet's nest you don't want to mess with."

"So why is this Storm Warrior so valuable to the Sioux?" Hunt asked.

"The Sioux think of him as a God," the Colonel answered. "He prays to his God every night, he teaches the young how to fight, and when he speaks the elders of the tribe listen. Until you spend some time with him, you'll never be able to understand it. But he has a lot of common sense, he's kind towards others; he encourages good will towards others, and when he gives his word it's done."

"There is no arrest warrant out for him, but I'd like to meet him," Hunt said. "I'd like to meet the man that so many think so highly of."

"I can arrange such a meeting," the Colonel said, "we can ride out tomorrow if you would like."

"Sounds good to me," Hunt answered. "I have to find out all I can about the missing scouts, so I may as well start with the Sioux."

Chapter 3

Visitors Arrive

U.S. Deputy Marshall Huntley Porter and Earl Jefferson were about to head out with Lt. Colonel Hawks and twenty soldiers when three white men arrived at the fort.

The strangers approached Lt. Colonel Hawks. "I am Charles Pollard," the older white haired man said.

Charles Pollard was a hard looking man, with cold blue eyes and the Colonel could tell he was used to getting his way.

"I am Judith's father, and I'm here to take my daughter and grandson home where they belong," he added.

Charles Pollard introduced his two traveling companions. "This is Burt Hanson, and this is Lance Fuller," Charles Pollard said as he glared at Lt. Colonel Hawks.

49

Hunt sized them up; Burt Hanson was a large muscular man, and Lance Fuller was a thin raw boned hard looking man with scars on his face and his scarred knuckles spoke for the number of skirmishes he's been in.

"I am Lt. Colonel Hawks, and this is U.S. Deputy Marshall Huntley Porter and Earl Jefferson, we are about to head out, what can I do for you?" Lt. Colonel Hawks asked.

"Like I said," Charles Pollard said as he glared back at Lt. Colonel Hawks, "I'm here to take my daughter Judith and her son home."

"Let's talk in the meeting room gentlemen," Lt. Colonel Hawks said as he started walking towards the meeting room.

Hunt, Earl, Captain Blanchard, Lieutenant Anderson and Sargent Black accompanied the men to the meeting room as the fort scouts, two men by the name of Griz and Slim fell in line and followed them in.

"This ought to be good," Slim said as he elbowed Griz and grinned.

After everyone was seated Lt. Colonel Hawks looked at Charles Pollard and began speaking.

"Mr. Pollard," Lt. Colonel Hawks said as he looked at him, "Your daughter Judith is married. She married a Sioux Chief by the name of Storm Warrior, and I will tell you right now that I will not allow you to force her to do anything that she doesn't want to do."

"I won't have my daughter living with savages and raising my grandson in a teepee and sleeping on dirt," Charles Pollard shouted back."

"Mr. Pollard," Lt. Colonel Hawks said, "they are not savages, and Judith married him on her own free will by a Methodist Minister here at the fort," the marriage is legal.

"I don't care if Jesus Christ himself married her," Charles Pollard blurted out," I'm taking my daughter and my grandson home."

"Mr. Pollard," Lt. Colonel Hawks said, "the Sioux are very intelligent and are ferocious fighters. Any of you that get out of line will be placed under arrest to prevent the Sioux from killing you."

"You must understand," Lt. Colonel Hawks continued, "her husband, Storm Warrior, is a mighty warrior and the other tribes fear him. Many stories are told of his feats in battle. He is a respected member of the Sioux Nation and anything less than respect will not be tolerated. Regardless of what you may think, he is a gentleman and treats Judith well."

"And you may as well leave your two bodyguards here," Lt. Colonel Hawks said as he glared at them, "if Storm Warrior wanted to he could easily kill them both if they get out of line. The Sioux are big on respect and won't tolerate disrespect. A wrong word and you could get us all killed."

"Yeah," Burt Hanson said as he twisted in his chair, "there were some Injuns a few days ago that thought so too, their bodies are rotting on the prairie now."

"They probably came to trade with you and you killed them," Lt. Colonel Hawks said as he glared at the large man. "There's a wagon train leaving Ft Smith that is due here anytime now. What you've done will anger the Indians and they'll be out for revenge and take it out on the wagon train."

"Yeah?" Burt said as he spat tobacco juice on the floor, "that's their problem, ain't it?" He said sarcastically.

"No, you fool," Lt. Colonel Hawks said, "Out here it's everyone's problem when a white man murders an Indian. They are a vengeful group; I'm amazed that they didn't track you down and kill you."

"We were plumb out of their neck of the woods by the time they found out," Burt continued, "we didn't leave any witnesses, hell, we even shot their puny looking horses."

"If it were a Sioux that you killed or a Pawnee you would be dead right now. I've seen them in action, and the three of you would be staked out on an anthill someplace screaming as the birds pluck the eyes from your head and the coyotes pull your guts out from the cut they make from your throat to your belly," Lt. Colonel Hawks said as he looked at the hate filled eyes of Burt Hanson.

"Mr. Pollard," the Colonel continued, "it would be in your best interest to leave these two idiots here when you go to see your daughter."

"They go where I go," Charles Pollard said sternly, "and I aim to take Judith back with me. I won't have my grandson raised by a bunch of Indians. And if there is trouble the Indians will find the three of us more than a match."

"Mr. Pollard," Lt. Colonel Hawks said, "like I told you, your daughter Judith and Storm Warrior are legally married and you will not force her to leave, my men and I will see to that. Second of all, she is in love with Storm Warrior, I could see it in her eyes and her actions when they were married. She is a schoolteacher in the Sioux Valley and teaches English to the young."

"Judith is under the protection of the entire Sioux nation and one cross word or any act of violence and the Sioux will bring down swift retribution. To escort her and her new husband from the fort to the Sioux Valley, they were accompanied by over twenty five hundred warriors. And that is only a portion of what they have in their main camp," Lt. Colonel Hawks explained.

"The Sioux are well-organized and obedient, they respect their elders. And when it comes to battles and planning attacks they are the best I've ever seen. Last spring the fort was under attack, then the Sioux showed up and the Sioux quickly put an end to the siege. In a matter of minutes they had overwhelmed and killed our attackers. Every man in this fort owes their lives to the Sioux, including me and I won't put up with any disrespect towards them, do you understand me?" Lt. Colonel Hawks asked.

"Yes," Charles Pollard said, "and I hope you understand me when I tell you I won't condone any disrespect from you or the redskins. When I get back, I plan to make a formal complaint with Washington regarding your attitude."

"Well that is good," the Colonel said, "because while you're filling out the papers you will be able to respond to the murder charges against you and your men for killing the Indians that your man Burt here was bragging about a short time ago in front of two U.S. Marshals and the C. O.of the fort that is trying to keep peace in this area."

"Yes," Charles Pollard said as he chuckled, "you do that. And when we tell them how we were brutally attacked, and we were forced to defend ourselves we will be regarded as heroes."

"Well," Lt. Colonel Hawks said with a sly smile, "that may be true, but just remember, you have to pass back through the land where you killed those Indians and this time their relatives may be waiting. And I won't risk the lives of my men to escort you and your two gun hands through hostile land."

"I will take you to the Sioux so you can see your daughter, but you need to leave these two men here," the Colonel said.

"No," Charles Pollard said, "I've already told you, where I go, they go. If you refuse to escort my two bodyguards and me then we will go by ourselves. I've traveled over two thousand miles, and I won't be turned back now."

"Very well," Lt. Colonel Hawks said, "but listen and listen well. If your so called bodyguards lift a rifle or pull their pistols my men behind them will have orders to shoot to kill, I will have them blown from their saddles, and leave them to rot on the prairie just as they left those Indians that came to trade and were murdered by you and your men."

"Your soldiers won't have a chance to shoot," Hunt said, "Earl and I will already have shot them before the soldier's clear leather."

Charles Pollard glared at Hunt, "Just whose side are you on, those filthy savages or an important business man with many contacts in Washington?"

"I believe in right and wrong," Hunt said, "what you plan on doing is wrong and I won't allow you or your two idiots to cause any problems."

"It is a two day ride by horseback," Lt. Colonel Hawks said as he cut in, Captain Blanchard and Sargent Black will accompany us, along with twenty soldiers, and the two scouts.

"Only twenty soldiers?" Charles Pollard asked.

"Yes," Lt. Colonel Hawks said, "the twenty are to protect the Sioux from you and your men starting anything, and the Sioux will protect us from attack by the other tribes."

"You seem to have a lot of confidence in the Sioux," Charles Pollard said.

"Yes, I do," Lt. Colonel Hawks answered, "and actually the Sioux will know we are coming the moment we cross the river into Sioux land and we will be met by a large group of warriors before we reach the halfway point to ask our intentions."

"Remember, Earl and I will ride along as well," Hunt said. "If there's any trouble we'll be there to handle it."

"OK," Lt. Colonel Hawks summed up, "we were preparing to leave for the Sioux camp just as you rode up. If you want to go then you may ride with us. But remember my warning about showing respect to the Sioux."

The next day Lt. Colonel Hawks was leading his men as they crossed the river after breaking camp.

As the soldiers traveled north at a walk the scout, Griz, yelled back at Lt. Colonel Hawks, "the Sioux know we're coming."

Everyone glanced towards the distant hills and saw the smoke signals.

"Yes," the Colonel said to Hunt, "within the hour they will have over a thousand warriors riding to meet us.

"Why so many?" Hunt asked.

"That's just the way the Sioux do things," the Colonel answered. "They don't start trouble, but when it appears they are ready."

At high noon the soldiers stopped to eat and rest the horses at a small creek. The two scouts reported seeing a few Sioux scouts in the distance.

"They're keeping an eye on us," Lt. Colonel Hawks responded, "they're waiting on the main force to arrive."

Lance Fuller was sitting on a rock and lit a rolled up cigarette with a twig from the small fire they had built.

Lt. Colonel Hawks didn't like the way Lance Fuller kept looking at him and asked him if he had a problem.

"Nope," Lance Fuller answered as he spat some tobacco from his mouth. "I was just thinking."

"Thinking about what?" The Colonel asked.

"I heard a story one time about how the Indians sometimes will fight for a woman. The winner gets the woman, and the loser gets a funeral. I was just wondering if I were to challenge this Storm Warrior to a duel and was to kill him then there wouldn't be anything to keep her from leaving the Indians and returning east with her father," Lance Fuller said with a smile.

Captain Blanchard tossed his almost empty coffee towards Lance and glared into his eyes. "You, against Storm Warrior? He'd have you and five more like you for lunch and not even raise a sweat."

"You have never seen me in action," Lance said as he glared at the Captain.

"You're right about that," Captain Blanchard said as he looked at Lance, "but I've seen him in action. We were under attack. I was wounded and was fighting off two attackers. Storm Warrior rode in and within seconds killed six enemies with his knife and save my life and the life of a young Private."

"I will guarantee you this," Captain Blanchard said, "you and Burt together couldn't whip him, and he'd kill you both so quick that your boss man here wouldn't even have time to light his fancy cigar."

"I've heard a few stories in my travels about this Storm Warrior," Hunt said. "Other tribes talk about him like he's a God or something. They say he catches arrows from the air."

"And once brought a storm that killed the enemy that was trying to get ahead of them and cut them off when they were outnumbered twenty to one. I just dismissed them as myth, something the Indians tell tall stories about," Hunt said.

"I don't believe in superstition," the Captain said, "but I do believe in the power of Storm Warrior. And so do the enemies of the Sioux. He's been challenged to a one on one duel a number of times, and from the stories I've heard he doesn't get a scratch or work up a sweat."

"So," Captain Blanchard said as he smiled, "seeing Lance here challenge Storm Warrior to a duel would be something I'd pay money to see."

"Like I said," Lance said, "you ain't ever seen me in action."

"No," the Colonel said as he walked up, "we haven't, but by the looks of the scars and skinned up knuckles it appears that you've gotten about the same as you've given. When you meet Storm Warrior you may notice he has no scars or skinned up knuckles, and I'll bet he's killed twenty or thirty in hand-to-hand battles. Something that I don't think you could say."

"Well," Lance said, "I can't wait to meet this feller."

"Yeah, me too," Burt said, "I'd like to see him stand nose to nose with me. Many a man has tried, but when it's over I'm the only one left standing."

"That's enough of this foolish talk," Lt. Colonel Hawks bellowed, "there will be no trouble from you two or, I'll have you put in irons, and I mean it. When we meet up with the Sioux, you will act respectfully and keep your mouths shut."

"What's the matter," Charles Pollard asked, "afraid this Storm Warrior can't handle himself?"

"Mr. Pollard," Lt. Colonel Hawks said as he stood up. "I honestly don't understand how a man so ignorant could have made a mark in his life like you have and still walk this earth."

"Your daughter has more class in her little finger than you do in your whole body. No wonder she traveled west to get away from you. You and your ways are why she is where she's at, don't you see it?" The Colonel asked.

"The only thing I see," Charles Pollard said menacingly as he stood and faced the Colonel, "is your incompetence in dealing with these savages. And when I return to Washington I can assure you changes will be made."

Knowing that arguing further with the likes of Charles Pollard would gain nothing the Colonel pulled the front brim of his hat down slightly, glared coldly at Pollard and said, "Mount up."

Lance and Burt smiled at each other; they knew their boss, Mr. Pollard, had gotten to the Colonel and were anxious to see what havoc he could bring down not only on the Colonel, but the Indians as well.

Hunt knew trouble was brewing and made up his mind to back the Colonel's move, whatever that turned out to be. And if backing his move meant shooting one or more of the three he was ready and willing to do it. He didn't like Charles Pollard for what he stood for, and disliked the two bodyguards even more.

Hunt was a very hard man; however, his seemingly mild manner fooled many into thinking he was not very aggressive. A number of criminals were in prison or buried as a result of misreading his ability.

He could draw and fire before most could even clear their holster, and he could hit a silver dollar at twenty five paces easily with the first shot. As everyone mounted to head out Hunt watched the two bodyguards closely, and the feelings he was getting from their body language troubled him. They intended to stir up trouble; he just didn't know when or how.

The two scouts rode out front with Sargent Black and were followed by the Colonel with Charles Pollard riding beside him. The two bodyguards followed next with Hunt and Earl riding behind them to watch their moves.

Hunt sensed that shooting the Colonel in the back and trying to blame it on the Indians would not be far from their realm of thought. This could cause the Army to respond and then Mr. Pollard would use the Army retrieve his daughter from the Indians.

Tension was high among the men as they rode north to meet the Sioux, everyone sensed it, especially the Colonel.

Chapter 4

JUDITH'S FATHER

L t. Colonel Hawks looked ahead and smiled when he saw Chief Gray Horse and Storm Warrior sitting on their horses waiting for the soldiers to approach.

"Well Mr. Pollard," the Colonel said as he looked ahead and saw Gray Horse and Storm Warrior waiting at the top of a hill ahead, "looks like you'll get to meet your son-in-law."

"What do you mean?" Charles Pollard asked, "One of those Indians is the one that took Judith?"

"The one on the right with the white hair is Storm Warrior, and the other is Chief Gray Horse, the smartest and mightiest War Chief of the plains. Remember to watch your manners, Chiefs of their ranking never travel alone, I would estimate up to two

63

thousand warriors are just over the hill and probably already have us surrounded," Lt. Colonel Hawks said.

"I thought you said they're friendly," Charles Pollard said sarcastically.

"They are, but they aren't stupid, that would be something for you to remember," Colonel Hawks answered.

Charles Pollard kept an eye on the two Indians and didn't see any sign of others. He was anxious to talk to the one called Storm Warrior and find the location of his daughter. After he got her back he would kill Storm Warrior if he had to, he was sure that if she had a choice between this Indian and her father that she would gladly return home with him.

"I don't like this," Lt. Colonel Hawks said to Charles Pollard.

"What do you mean?" Charles Pollard asked.

"Don't you realize we just rode into a trap?" Lt. Colonel Hawks asked, "Be extra attentive of your language, one wrong word or anyone fires a weapon and we'll all be dead in minutes."

Charles Pollard turned in his saddle and spoke to his two bodyguards. "Keep them holstered boys, don't start anything here."

"Wise words," the Colonel said under his breath.

"Nice looking horses those Indians have," Charles Pollard said just loud enough for the Colonel to hear.

"Yes," the Colonel said, "they are."

The column came to a halt, and the Colonel rode forward to greet Chief Gray Horse and Storm Warrior with Charles Pollard stayed next to him.

"Greetings Gray Horse, greetings Storm Warrior," the Colonel said with a smile as Charles Pollard came to a stop next to the Colonel.

Without returning his greeting Gray Horse looked at Charles Pollard and asked, "who is he and why is he here?"

Before Lt. Colonel Hawks could speak, Charles Pollard introduced himself. "I am Charles Pollard; I am Judith's father, and I have come to take her home. I trust that she is safe and unharmed," he said menacingly.

Storm Warrior rode his pony forward a few steps and glared into Charles Pollards eyes, "she is my wife, and she will stay."

"Yeah," Charles Pollard said, "we'll see about that."

The tones of Charles Pollard's words were unfriendly, and this was the signal for the others to appear.

65

Five hundred warriors following Gray Horse appeared as they rode their ponies up the hill and formed a semi-circle around the Colonel and Mr. Pollard. At the same time, both sides of the rise were filled with warriors, led by Chief Gray Wolf and Chief Red Elk.

The soldiers began looking all around them, and realized they were greatly outnumbered, so they remained relaxed. The two bodyguards became nervous, and Lance unsnapped his pistol holster.

"Leave it where it is or I'll blow a hole through the back of your head," Captain Blanchard said.

"I insist on seeing my daughter," Charles Pollard said. "I received a letter from her, she said her husband was attacked and killed, and she was taken prisoner. She asked me to come and get her."

"Blackfeet killed her husband and others at the Northern pass last fall," Storm Warrior said. "Judith stayed at the fort with the others. We were married at the fort by the religious man, and she came to live with me here. She was not made a prisoner, and she did not ask you to come get her. This morning she told me she wanted to give me a son."

This comment irked Charles Pollard. He couldn't imagine his daughter trying to get pregnant by a savage.

"Are you calling me a liar?" Charles Pollard asked angrily?

"Yes, your words are not the true," Storm Warrior said. "I can read the white man's words, show me this letter," he continued."

"Well, I, uh, left it at home. Take me to my daughter, she will tell you," Charles Pollard answered.

Storm Warrior looked at Gray Horse; Gray Horse nodded and then Storm Warrior said, "I will take you to your daughter and then you will leave and never come back."

"Oh, I will return, and I'll bring plenty of support, you can bank on that," Charles Pollard said.

"Then you will die," Storm Warrior said as he gazed into Charles Pollard's eyes.

"You," Gray Horse said, as he caught Charles Pollard's attention. "You and two others rode through the Shoshone land six suns ago?"

"He means six days ago," the Colonel said.

"Yes, I was traveling but I don't know anything about it being Shoshone Land. It belongs to the United States of America," Charles Pollard answered.

"My scouts read smoke signals from the Shoshone to the Pawnee. They are searching for three-white men pulling two pack

67

animals that killed three-young Shoshone boys that were no more than ten winters old. They left to go hunting rabbits with their bows and arrows and never came home," Gray Horse said.

"Shoshone warriors followed the sign of the buzzards and found the three young braves dead from many bullets and their ponies were shot," Gray Horse said.

"We were attacked," Charles Pollard said, "we were defending ourselves."

"Young boys hunting rabbits don't attack armed men," Gray Horse said.

"Are you calling me a liar?" Charles Pollard asked.

"Yes, I am saying you killed those three young braves," Gray Horse said. "I think you will find murdering Sioux children a little more difficult."

"Mr. Pollard," the Colonel said sternly, "I will remind you to watch your manners. We are guests of the Sioux, and I ask that you focus on your mission here or I will have you arrested and taken back to the fort."

Charles Pollard looked at Gray Horse, "I apologize, I came to see my daughter. Would you please take me to her?"

"We will travel to the springs," Gray Horse said, "there your soldiers and men can wait. I will take you and the Colonel to the camp to see Judith."

"Where I go, my bodyguards go," Charles Pollard said belligerently.

"Then leave," Gray Horse said, "you are not welcome here."

"I came to see my daughter," Charles Pollard said as he raised his voice, "and you cannot stop me!"

"You leave, or you die," Gray Horse said unmoved by his angry voice.

Charles Pollard realized he was losing the argument; he could tell by the Indian's body language that he was about to be blown from his saddle as Gray Horse leveled his rifle across his ponies neck and pointed it at his chest.

Charles Pollard glanced from Gray Horse to Storm Warrior, and saw no mercy in either of their faces.

Just then attention was drawn to the sound of a horse walking up to the Colonel and Mr. Pollard. Attention was drawn to the man with the star on his shirt.

"I am U.S. Marshall Huntley Porter; I traveled here from Denver," he said looking at Gray Horse, "I couldn't help but

69

overhear the conversation. I would like permission to visit your camp and speak to Mrs. Storm Warrior."

"If she is happy and wants to stay then she shall stay. I understand she has established a school for the Indians, and I think that is an honorable and respectable thing to do," Hunt said.

"Mr. Pollard and his two cronies are a little short on manners and I will report their actions to my superiors when I return to Denver," Hunt said. "Chief Gray Horse, do I have your permission to come to the Sioux camp and speak to the schoolteacher?"

"I sense," Gray Horse said, "that you are an honorable man, my warriors will take you to see Judith if her husband allows it."

"And what about me?" Charles Pollard said, "I've traveled over two thousand miles to see my daughter and I can't turn back now."

"You may come if Storm Warrior allows it, but your men cannot. They will remain at the springs with the soldiers," Gray Horse said.

"OK, if that's how it has to be then so be it. How about it Storm Warrior," Charles Pollard asked, "you going to let me see my daughter or are you afraid of what she may say?"

"You, the Colonel, and the Marshal may come if my War Chief allows it," Storm Warrior said. "But it is the Sioux customs that if you speak with disrespect to my wife that I kill you. I will not allow you to speak to her as you have spoken to me."

"I'll be there," Hunt said, "if he gets out of line I will handle him."

"And I will cut out his tongue," Storm Warrior said as he stared into Charles Pollard's cold blue eyes.

"Chief Gray Horse," Hunt said, "I have traveled here with another U.S. Deputy Marshal, may he come with us as well?"

"Yes," Gray Horse answered as Earl rode his horse up next to Hunt and smiled to Gray Horse.

"Storm Warrior," Lt. Colonel Hawks said, "Captain Blanchard would like to see the colt you have promised him, would it be OK to allow him to come so he can see the colt?"

"Yes," Gray Horse answered, "but no more."

"Come," Gray Horse said, "we will take you to the springs where the soldiers can wait. He turned his pony and the Colonel with Charles Pollard riding close followed Gray Horse and Storm Warrior. The soldiers followed next with the Indians on both sides of them.

It was evening when they arrived; the Colonel glanced at his watch, it was 5:15 PM. They arrived at the springs, and they were told they could camp here.

71

The soldiers would remain and the two bodyguards rode up to Charles Pollard. "You boys will stay here and keep the soldier boys company until I come back," Charles Pollard told them.

"I thought you said where you go, we go," Burt said to him.

"Not this time boys," Charles Pollard said, "You two stay here and keep your mouths shut. Sounds like I may spend the night so remain calm and don't start any trouble and I'll be back either late tonight or tomorrow."

"Sargent Black," Lt. Colonel Hawks said, "I am leaving you in charge. Captain Blanchard and I will ride to the Sioux Camp. Don't let anyone wander away from camp, understand?"

"I understand sir," Sargent Black said as he saluted.

The two bodyguards watched as Charles Pollard, Hunt, Earl, Lt. Colonel Hawks and Captain Blanchard rode away with the Indians.

Sargent Black ordered camp to be made. Everyone dismounted and loosened their saddles before removing them. The horses were allowed to drink and graze on the lush grass around the spring. A fire was built, and soon card games were being played.

The bodyguards didn't like being left behind. They thought the soldier boys were boring, and they didn't like taking orders from the Sargent.

And they didn't like the Indians keeping an eye on them either. With nothing else to do they loosened the saddles but left them on the horses. Then they sauntered over to where a few were starting a card game and settled down until they heard from their boss.

"Take the saddles off your horses," Sargent Black ordered, "they'll get sores on their backs if you leave them on."

Reluctantly they removed the saddles and sat on a log as they glared at the Sargent.

Charles Pollard wasn't expecting so many Indians, nor was he counting on them being so set in their ways or being friends with the Colonel at the fort. Charles Pollard's strategy about killing the Indian married to his daughter would have to wait.

Hunt took note that after leaving the soldiers and the other men at the springs Gray Horse left a thousand of his warriors to keep an eye on the soldier's camp. The warriors were placed almost a half mile above the soldier's camp. The soldiers weren't Gray Horse's concern, however, the two that traveled with Charles Pollard were.

Gray Horse climbed a steep hill and then cut in between two slabs of rock, suddenly they found themselves in a narrow crevice and water was trickling down the trail they were traveling.

Gray Horse noticed the wolves in the rocks and timbers above but not wanting to tip the visitors off didn't acknowledge them.

After a short time, they broke out onto the valley floor of the central Sioux camp. Storm Warrior quickly caught up with him and once again they fell into line two abreast.

Gray Horse and Storm Warrior mounted the rise and then it was downhill to the main camp.

Hunt and Earl were amazed at the sight they saw as they topped a small hill and started down towards the village when suddenly Charles Pollard shouted Judith's name and kicked his horse into a run.

Charles Pollard had noticed a wooden structure that appeared to resemble a schoolhouse. When he saw it, he cried out Judith's name and kicked his horse into a full run.

No one was expecting him to act so foolishly, and immediately Storm Warrior kicked his horse into a run and quickly caught him, Charles Pollard took a swing at Storm Warrior, so Storm Warrior had no choice but knock him from his horse with a blow to his neck.

Charles Pollard landed hard and rolled to a stop. As he was getting up he looked up and Storm Warrior was standing over him. It angered him that the one married to his daughter was the one that knocked him from his horse.

"I've traveled over two thousand miles to see my daughter, and you can't stop me!" He shouted as he stood up.

"You will see my wife when I allow it," Storm Warrior said as the others rode up and stopped.

"Mr. Pollard," the Colonel shouted, "what do you think you're doing?"

"I'm going to see my daughter, what the hell do you think I'm doing," Charles Pollard shouted back.

"You fool," the Colonel shouted, "they will bring your daughter to you when they are ready. Storm Warrior is her husband, no man may speak to a Sioux woman without her husband's permission, and you need to get that into your head."

"Yea, well she's my daughter, or have you forgotten that?" Charles Pollard asked.

"She may have been your daughter once," Storm Warrior said, "but now she is my wife, and she is conducting class."

Charles Pollard walked over and picked up his hat and put it on and brushed himself off. He was red in the face and walked towards Storm Warrior and said, "I will see her right now!"

Hunt watched as Charles Pollard approached Storm Warrior with a snarl on his lips as he spoke harshly. Storm Warrior kicked him in a sweeping round kick to the head, and Charles Pollard fell in a heap, he was knocked out cold.

"That was fast," Earl said to Hunt.

"Yes," Hunt said, "but it was a poor kick, looks like his head is still attached."

Several warriors came and they threw Charles Pollard over his horse and then they rode to the teepee reserved for guests. Charles Pollard's gun was removed and given to the Colonel.

Lt. Colonel Hawks apologized to Gray Horse and Storm Warrior, but Gray Horse was in no mood, Gray Horse was angry.

When they arrived at the teepee Gray Horse pushed Charles Pollard from his horse with his foot as he crashed to the ground.

"He has to be the rudest man I have ever met," Hunt said to the Colonel as he dismounted.

"Yes," the Colonel said, "and the dumbest too."

"You will stay here," Gray Horse said, "when the council meets we will come get you," he said to Lt. Colonel Hawks, Captain Blanchard, Hunt and Earl.

Twelve warriors were left to keep an eye on them; the horses taken for water and food.

Lt. Colonel Hawks, Captain Blanchard, Hunt and Earl carried Charles Pollard into the teepee and dropped him on the floor.

Water and food were brought just as Charles Pollard began coming to.

He was holding his head and moaning, "I'll kill that son-of-a-bitch for hitting me he said."

"Yeah," Hunt said, "you did a real good job of showing him who was boss."

"Don't get smart with me Marshal," Charles Pollard said, "I'll have you fired."

"You, Mr. Pollard, don't worry me one bit," Hunt said.

"What the hell where you thinking when you took off running like that?" Lt. Colonel Hawks asked.

"I was going to see my daughter, what the hell do you think? I could see the school; I knew she would be there," Charles Pollard answered.

"She's been gone for three years. She married that rift-raft army sargent. Then he came out west where he got himself killed, and I aim to take her and my grandson back with me and that damned Redskin isn't going to stop me," Charles Pollard said.

"If you haven't figured it out yet," Hunt said, "you aren't doing anything that those Injuns won't allow you to do. You and your impertinent methods will get you nowhere. Time to use your head and show them a little respect, and then they may even let you see your daughter."

"Hunt is right," the Colonel said. "Your arrogance could get you killed. Tonight when they come to get us we will be taken to a large lodge, the highest-ranking Chiefs from both camps will be there. Don't for a minute think they are a bunch of ignorant Indians. The older Chiefs are very wise. It's the Indian version of Congress. You'll be asked why you want to see your daughter and any sign of disrespect will get you in big trouble. If you want to see your daughter, you'd better be watching your manners."

"And you don't speak until asked to speak. Some don't speak English so someone may be repeating what you say in Sioux, so the others know what is being said," Lt. Colonel Hawks said. "You need to know that a little over two years ago a Chief shot his own son because his son was disrespectful and went against customs. If a Sioux would shoot his own son, believe me, they would have no trouble telling you to get out and never come back, and if you do they would have no trouble killing you."

"Storm Warrior would have been justified if he killed you today, you're lucky all he did was knock you from your horse and kick you in the head," Hunt said.

78

The Colonel was holding his pistol and the Marshals were armed, Charles Pollard knew he was out of options at the moment.

"Well," Charles Pollard said, "with the Colonel holding my pistol and the security guards out front I don't really have a choice, do I? But, when I get back to Philadelphia changes will be made. The entire prairie will be wiped clean of redskins and the land will become farmland, the Shoshone, Blackfeet, Cheyenne, and the Sioux to start. And we'll have an army here to round them up and put them in the reservation, the ones that live that is."

"And I can make sure certain individuals have a nice bounty on their head, if you know what I mean," Charles Pollard said.

"You know," Hunt said as he looked at Charles Pollard, "there's a side of me that hopes the Shoshone catch up to you on your way back."

"Yeah," the Colonel said as he smiled, "maybe a little birdie might tell of your travel plans."

"I'd like to know why you're so bitter towards everyone," Lt. Colonel Hawks said as he looked at Charles Pollard, "you are filled with so much hate I honestly don't know how anyone can stand to work with you or be your friend. Trusting you would be like trusting a rattlesnake or a wild animal, one day they will turn on you, just as I'm sure one day you turn on them."

Charles Pollard looked at the Colonel menacingly but didn't say anything. He was quite irritated as he said, "yeah, just keep blabbering, does you more good to say it than it does me to hear it."

"And you have a beautiful daughter; she must take after your wife," Captain Blanchard said, "There is no way a woman like her could take after you. She's smart, kind, and has a way with people. I've heard the Indian kids love her, and she loves them. She doesn't care about your money or what you can do for her."

"She once told me in confidence," Lt. Colonel Hawks said, "that you controlled her and made her life miserable. All she could think about was getting as far away from you as she could so she decided to get married and move to Oregon with her husband."

"Yeah, that was a decision that could have gotten her killed," Charles Pollard said. "She comes west; she's pregnant, has a baby in the back of a wagon, spends all winter in a small cabin by herself with a baby, and now she's living here among savages."

"Yeah," Lt. Colonel Hawks said, "and she appears very happy."

"Happy? How the hell can anyone be happy living here, like this?" Charles Pollard asked.

"Well," the Colonel said, "if the Sioux don't kick you out you may spend a few days here and see how happy they are."

"They're a well-organized group," Lt. Colonel Hawks said, "everyone has duties to perform; boys learn to fight and hunt, girls help with the cooking and raising the little ones. Everyone watches everyone else's child, and their herds of horses are kept under the watchful eye by the braves on horseback."

"Scouts cover every entrance into the valley, and scouts are out on the plains and are constantly sending messages back to the main camp," Captain Blanchard added.

"Everyone reports to someone and everyone does their job with no complaining and no questions. It's a matter of honor," Lt. Colonel Hawks said, "the Indians place a lot of importance on respect and honor."

"Honor," Charles Pollard said disgustedly as he stood and walked to the door and looked out, "these savages don't even recognize the term."

"That's where you're wrong," the Colonel said as he watched Charles Pollard. "Their culture is built on respect and honor."

"When a Sioux gives his word you can bet on it. And when a Sioux says no, he means no, and if someone goes against his decision he'd better be willing to fight or die," Lt. Colonel Hawks said.

"Yeah," Charles Pollard said, "that pleases me. That means there will be a lot of dead Indians."

"You, Mr. Pollard," Hunt said, "are the sorriest son-of-a-bitch I've ever seen. When I return to Denver, I plan to file a complete report regarding the murder of those ten-year old Shoshone boys. I'm sure the Secretary of Indian affairs or the Attorney General will have a few questions for you."

"Yeah," Charles Pollard said as he looked back at Hunt, "and I'll be written up as a hero after I tell them we were attacked and were defending ourselves."

"Children attacked you? And you expect educated men to believe that?" Hunt asked.

"It doesn't matter what they believe," Charles Pollard said. "If they expect loans and support from other Politicians to further their careers they'll make the obvious decision. And decisions will be made about both of your careers; it wouldn't surprise me to see you both called back to Washington to stand trial and answer why you allowed a highly respected member of the elite to be beaten and held captive while your hand picked replacements will come to take over and put these redskins in their place."

"Like I said earlier," Hunt said, "you don't scare me. And I could care less about my work as a U.S. Deputy Marshall. However, since I was recommended by a highly respected U.S.

Marshal to come west and take this job you may have a difficult time when it comes to believing who's telling the truth under oath."

"And the same goes for me," the Colonel said. "I met with President Fillmore five years ago prior to taking this job. He asked me to come west and establish a relationship with the Indians, and I've been sending detailed reports back to Washington on a weekly basis complete with dates, names and occurrences."

"I have a letter in my desk written by President Pierce dated only a month ago commending me for the progress we've made with the Indians and to keep up the good work," Lt. Colonel Hawks said, "Now I'm sure the President and the Secretary of War will be anxious to know why you killed three ten-year old boys out hunting rabbits. And you may find some of your, so called friends in high places, may be reluctant to stick their necks out when they find out how pissed the Secretary of War and the President of the United States is with your actions and attitude."

"So keep showing your winning personality and if you make it out of here alive and the Shoshone don't find you on your return trip I hope you'll have some free time to travel to Washington and answer the charges of murder and attempts at instigating trouble between the Indians and the whites," Lt. Colonel Hawks said.

"Your threats don't scare me," Charles Pollard said as he glared at the Colonel, "those Indians attacked us, and we were defending ourselves."

"I'll tell you this," Hunt said as he flipped his cigarette away, "you cause trouble here, and I will arrest you and put you in irons and you'll travel back to Denver with me."

"You wouldn't dare," Charles Pollard said under his breath in a threatening manner.

"Just try me," Hunt answered as he glared back.

"My men would never allow it" Charles Pollard said, "They will kill you."

"It's funny you should mention them," Hunt said, "cause I would plan to take them back with you, and with a little luck the three of you could be spending some quality time together in a Federal Prison."

"You don't know my men," Charles Pollard said, "there's no way you would be able to put them in irons. Denver is a long trip and many things can happen on the trail. I don't think you'd want to try and pull off something like that."

"If it comes to that," the Colonel said, "I'd send a detail back to Denver with the Marshals to make sure you get there safely. So if I were you I'd realize you're in our backyard now and try to behave yourself."

"I hope you're as compassionate when Judith returns with us," Charles Pollard answered.

"And just what makes you think she'd return with you?" The Colonel asked.

"She's my daughter, and she's being held here against her will," Charles Pollard answered.

"She's not here against her will," Lt. Colonel Hawks said, "she's here because she asked to come and she truly loves Storm Warrior and a Methodist Minister at the fort married them."

"Yeah?" Charles Pollard answered with a snarl on his lips, "just wait until I get her alone and can talk to her; you'll see her change her tune real quick."

"First of all," Hunt said, "you won't get her alone so you can threaten and intimidate her. And if you get out of line I'll personally whack you over the head with my pistol and you'll wake up bound and gagged, headed for Denver."

"You sir," Charles Pollard said disgustedly, "Are a disgrace to the United States of America."

"And you sir," Hunt said as he coldly stared into his eyes, "are a disgrace to the human race."

"I will caution you that when you speak to Judith to speak with respect," the Colonel added, "she is a full-grown, mature

85

woman, and she is married to an important Sioux chief. Her husband is fearless and could kill you in an instant."

The four of them left the teepee and stood outside looking down towards the camp leaving Charles Pollard sitting alone in the teepee.

Fires were lit in the camp and drums were beating a steady rhythm.

"That's quite a sight," Hunt said to Earl as he looked over the Sioux camp. "I'd love to walk among them and speak to them."

"Maybe you will have that opportunity," Lt. Colonel Hawks said.

The Sioux guards watched as Hunt rolled a cigarette and lit it. Just then a large party of Sioux rode past the teepee led by several Chiefs dressed in their finest.

"These are the Sioux from the northern tribe," the Colonel explained as they watched them ride by. "All-important tribal decisions are made with all Chiefs present."

"They're a magnificent looking group," Hunt said as he watched them riding by.

"I see pride and confidence in their faces," Earl added.

"Well," Charles Pollard said as he came from the teepee and watched them riding by, "you make them sound like model citizens. Maybe you can explain to me why they're always at war with each other and why wagon trains are attacked and everyone, including women and children are killed."

"The Blackfeet attacked the wagon train, not the Sioux," the Colonel answered. "I can't explain why that happened, but it was the Sioux that accompanied us back to the site of the attack and protected us while we retrieved what was left."

And later as we were returning to the fort we were attacked by a large Blackfeet force and if it wasn't for the Sioux we would have all been killed," Captain Blanchard said.

Then Gray Horse walked to the campsite, "the council is waiting for you, "follow me."

The Colonel nodded, and the men followed Gray Horse down to the main camp. The crowd parted and allowed them to pass. Charles Pollard followed the Colonel, Captain Blanchard, Hunt and Earl followed as they kept an eye on Charles Pollard.

"Weapons are not allowed inside the council lodge," Gray Horse said as he turned at the entrance and faced them. "The guards will keep your weapons until you leave."

The Colonel, Captain Blanchard, Hunt and Earl handed over their weapons and then followed Gray Horse inside.

A wide space was left at the far end of the circle and the Colonel approached and sat down.

Charles Pollard looked around, there were several solemn faces staring at him; he looked at the Chiefs that were seated and didn't see Judith.

Seeing the Colonel take a seat he figured that he was expected to sit, so he took a seat next to the Colonel and Captain Blanchard, then Hunt and Earl sat on the other side of Charles Pollard.

Gray Horse had told Red Bear and the other chiefs about the trouble they had with him earlier in the day and about Storm Warrior kicking him in the head and knocking him off his horse.

Knowing that he was Judith's father was the only reason they had allowed him to sit in the lodge with the leaders of the Sioux and hear what he had to say.

The chiefs had asked Storm Warrior to bring Judith to the lodge and to wait outside until she was asked to come in so all could hear what would be said. Red Bear looked at the five white men and after what would be considered a respectable time picked up the pipe and lit it.

He puffed on the pipe and passed it around; no one spoke; all were quite as the pipe was passed. Charles Pollard didn't see Storm Warrior and wondered where he was.

The pipe made its way back to Chief Red Bear, and just as he was placing it back in its cradle the flap to the lodge was opened and Storm Warrior entered; he walked around the council chiefs and stood next to Gray Horse.

He stood and crossed his arms and looked at Red Bear as the light from the fire reflected off of his white hair. Charles Pollard was growing impatient but waited. Finally, Red Bear looked at the Colonel and spoke.

"Colonel," Red Bear spoke in Sioux, "the Sioux are honored to have the white Colonel visit their camp. A translator repeated what Red Bear said in English.

The Colonel waited until the translator was finished and then he told Red Bear how glad he was to see his good friends again. Once again the translator repeated in Sioux what was said.

Charles Pollard was a pro at winning in a political setting, and as he looked around he realized he was in just such a setting, and he figured it was time to put on his warm political front to achieve what he has set out to do. Besides, he figured, he'd have these ignorant savages eating out of his hand in no time.

Red Bear stared at Charles Pollard and the U.S. Marshals and waited.

Lt. Colonel Hawks realized he was waiting for an introduction.

"Red Bear," the Colonel said, "forgive me for my lack of manners. May I introduce Mr. Charles Pollard from Philadelphia?

89

Mr. Pollard is a very successful banker and has many political contacts in Washington. He is also Judith's father and has ridden many miles to see her."

The interpreter repeated the introduction and everyone stared at Charles Pollard.

"Why do you come?" Red Bear asked Charles Pollard. The interpreter translated to Charles Pollard what was said.

"I received a letter from my daughter," Charles Pollard said.

"She said Indians had killed her husband, and she wanted to come home. I have ridden over two thousand miles to find my daughter and bring her home," Charles Pollard answered and waited for Red Bear's answer as the interpreter translated.

Red Bear stared into Charles Pollards eyes as the interpreter repeated what he had said and then ignored him as he stared at Hunt and Earl.

"And this, Chief Red Bear," Lt. Colonel Hawks said, "is U.S. Deputy Marshall Huntley Porter and Earl Jefferson from Denver. They asked to ride along and hear what Judith has to say about living here with the Sioux."

After the translator finished Hunt said, "And if she's happy here then I'll see to it that she stays," he said as he looked at

90

Charles Pollard. Hunt waited for the interpreter to finish before continuing.

"Also," Hunt said, "I was sent to find out what had happened to two army scouts that disappeared last year. Did they visit your tribe?" Hunt waited until the translator finished.

"Two traders came one summer before, but they left and traveled west. They did not say they were army scouts," Red Bear answered. The interpreter repeated what was said and then Hunt continued.

"Did they say where they were headed?" Hunt asked.

"No," Red Bear answered after the translator finished. "They spoke of the white man's yellow iron and asked if we knew where they could find some, but we told them we did not know, they acted angry and insulted us; they were ordered to leave and they left. They were told to never return, or they would die." The interpreter repeated what was said to the others.

"Could some of your warriors take me on the trail that they took when they left your camp?" Hunt asked.

"Why do you want to follow their trail?" Red Bear asked.

"I need to find them," Hunt answered, "if they are alive I need to arrest them and bring them to Denver to stand trial for desertion, among other charges. And if they're dead I need to find their bodies." Red Bear waited for the interpreter to finish.

91

"My warriors will only take you as far as the land of the Blackfeet," Red Bear said, "we are at peace with the Blackfeet as long as they stay on their land and we stay on our land. I cannot guarantee your safety if you enter the land of the Blackfeet. They are the ones that attacked the wagon train and their word of peace cannot be trusted."

After the translator finished Hunt said, "I understand, any help your warriors can give me would be greatly appreciated, and your support will be reported to my superiors." Once again everyone waited until the interpreter had completed.

"I came to see my daughter," Charles Pollard blurted out, "I realize she is here, when can I see her?"

The translator repeated what he had said.

"Judith is Storm Warrior's squaw," Red Bear said as he gestured towards him, "she teaches English to the young in the schoolhouse that the white soldiers constructed. She is happy, our people speak highly of her and our young bring her gifts."

As the interpreter repeated what was said, Charles Pollard gathered his wits about him to persuade the chief to allow him to speak to his daughter.

"Yes," Charles Pollard said, "she's always been able to win people over. She has a winning personality, and I put her through college. I'm sure she's doing a marvelous job of teaching; that has always been her passion. I just want to speak to her and make sure she is OK and find out if she needs anything. Her mother, and I are both very worried about her."

After the interpreter finished Red Bear spoke, "earlier you said that she wrote you a letter and that she wanted you to come and bring her home."

"Yes, that is true," Charles Pollard said. The interpreter quickly repeated what had just been said.

"I think you don't speak the truth," Red Bear said. "A woman that wants her father to come get her will not marry a Sioux and build a school to teach."

Charles Pollard's patience was growing thin.

This Indian had just seen through his smoke screen and had called him a liar.

"I think," Charles Pollard said as he coldly stared at Red Bear, "that it would be in the Sioux's best interest if they allowed me to take my daughter home."

Red Bear stared into his eyes while the interpreter translated what had just been said.

"I think," Red Bear said as he stared back at Charles Pollard, "that it is time for all to hear what Judith has to say." He motioned to Storm Warrior and Storm Warrior walked to the flap and held it open as Judith entered.

Charles Pollard started to get up, but the Colonel grabbed his arm and told him to be still. He looked angrily at the Colonel as Hunt grabbed his other arm and said, "You heard him, sit still and mind your manners."

Charles Pollard settled down and watched as Judith walked with Storm Warrior to stand before the council chiefs.

She looked at her father, smiled and said, "Hello father."

Red Bear spoke, "your father claims he has come to take you home. He says that you wrote him a letter, and you asked him to come and take you home. Is this correct?"

"It is true that I did write him a letter," Judith answered. "I told him about my husband being killed and that I was marrying Storm Warrior. I wrote that I was going to teach the Sioux's young and that the soldiers were building a school on the Sioux land. But I did not ask him to come and get me. I think that my work here is too important to leave." The interpreter repeated what was said.

"You married Storm Warrior by the white man of God at the fort and again by Sioux law so that all would know that you belong to Storm Warrior. Do you want to leave your husband and return with your father?" Red Bear asked.

94

"Oh no," Judith answered, "I love my husband and I love the Sioux. Everyone treats me with great respect; I've never been happier."

"Then you want to stay?" Red Bear asked. "Of course," she said, "I couldn't leave my husband or the Sioux."

"And I have much work to do here, the Sioux children are obedient, loving and learn so fast. I never knew until I came here how much I would love them, and I have been treated with love and respect," she added. The interpreter repeated and then was quiet.

Everyone had eyes on Charles Pollard. Everyone heard what Judith had to say and waited to hear what the white man had to say. But, to everyone's surprise it was Hunt that spoke first.

"Judith, I am U.S. Marshall Huntley Porter, and this is U.S. Marshal Earl Jefferson on assignment from Denver to locate two missing army scouts. I visited the fort when your father and two other men rode in, and I heard they were coming to the Sioux camp so I asked if I could travel with them." Hunt waited until the interpreter was completed before continuing.

"Your father sounded convinced that you were here against your wishes by a letter you had written him. He told the Colonel and myself that he was coming here to take you and your son back east with him," Hunt said and waited for the interpreter to finish translating.

"Thinking there may be trouble I rode along to hear what you had to say and see for myself the conditions of how you are living and the circumstances of your marriage to Storm Warrior." The interpreter began repeating what had been said and when he was finished Hunt continued.

"Did you willingly marry Storm Warrior?"

"Yes," Judith answered, "I love and respect him very much. The interpreter quickly stated what was asked and then Hunt continued.

"Did you willingly come to the Sioux camp?"

"Yes," she answered, "teaching is what I've wanted to do ever since I was a little girl."

The interpreter quickly finished and then Hunt asked, "How do you feel about having a chance to return with your father?"

Judith turned to look at her father and said, "Father, I think of you and mother every day. I love you both very much, and I thank you for all that you've done for me, including my education. But I've found my purpose in life, and this is what I was born to do."

"I've never been happier," Judith said as she continued, "If I were forced to leave the Sioux camp and return home it would break my heart. I love it here; I love teaching the children, I love the people, I love watching them work and play, the people support each other, and I love watching my husband working with the young men, and I can see the love and respect in their eyes when they speak to him."

"To answer your question Marshall Porter," Judith said as she turned and looked at him, "there is no way I would leave my life here, besides loving my husband more than I ever thought was possible to love another, I love the Sioux people, the children and my duty here."

Hunt turned his head, and glared at Charles Pollard while he waited for the interpreter to finish.

"Your words are music to my ears," Hunt said as he looked at Judith, "and I will put it in my journal and will forward it to Washington. It is obvious that you are content and happy, and to hear someone say how much one loves their job is a pleasant change." The interpreter took advantage of the pause to translate.

"As far as I am concerned you have nothing to worry about, if anyone forces you to leave or harms you in any way I would hunt them down," Hunt said.

"When you find them," Storm Warrior said, "you would just get their body, I would get there first." Quickly the translator repeated and waited.

"And as her husband you would have every right under the law to protect her, I respect you for that," Hunt said, "If I had a wife, I would do the same. I'm sure that after hearing Judith speak, Mr. Pollard knows that his trip here was wasted, and now he has two thousand miles to travel to return home content knowing that his daughter is very satisfied. Isn't that right Mr. Pollard?" Hunt said as he looked at him. The translator repeated what was said and waited.

Charles Pollard looked around and knew that he had to be careful about what he said, the warning from Storm Warrior was meant for him and he knew it. And he knew that the U.S. Marshall would put him under arrest if he tried anything, so he was left with little choice.

"Yes," Charles Pollard said in response to the Marshal's topic. "However I don't think my trip was wasted, I got to see my daughter for the first time in over three-years, and I look forward to seeing my grandson before I leave."

"I would ask permission from the Sioux to allow me a few days to watch my grandson play and be able to spend some quality time with my daughter and watch her teach," Charles Pollard said. "I would like to see for myself the life my daughter has made for herself and try to understand why she loves living here among the Sioux so much."

"If Storm Warrior allows it," Red Bear said as he stared coldly at Charles Pollard.

Eyes turned to Storm Warrior, and he looked at Charles Pollard as he spoke. "Only if you are not armed and you obey what you are told and do not go where you are told not to go, you will have an escort of warriors with you at all times," Storm Warrior said.

"Can my men join me here in the Sioux camp?" Charles Pollard asked.

"No," Storm Warrior said, "I do not like them; I think they would cause trouble and I would have to kill them."

"I promise not to cause any trouble," Charles Pollard answered, "I hardly think the escorts would be necessary."

"Thinking you would not create trouble is the reason I will allow you to remain for two days," Storm Warrior answered. "On the third morning we will escort you back to your men, and you will leave the land of the Sioux forever and not return."

"Very well," Charles Pollard said, "two days." His mind was thinking fast, and he knew he was given two days to convince Judith to return east with him.

The Colonel spoke up, "I will need to return to where my men are camped and tell them about the delay in returning Red Bear."

"I will have warriors escort you back to the springs where your men are camped," Red Bear answered.

"I would like permission to stay here," Hunt said, "and perhaps your warriors could show me the trail that the scouts took when they left your camp."

"I will discuss that with the other chiefs after this meeting is over and we will let you know our decision," Red Bear answered.

"Fair enough Red Bear," Hunt answered, "any help you can give us will be greatly appreciated."

Chapter 5

SATAN SHOWS HIMSELF

After the meeting the white men were led outside. Storm Warrior escorted Judith and immediately Charles Pollard took her in his arms and they hugged.

"How is mother doing?" Judith asked.

"She misses you," Charles Pollard answered, "and she wants you to come home. We need to talk," he said.

Just then Sun Bird appeared from the crowd with Matt and Ghost.

"Father," Judith said, "I want you to meet Matthew, your Grandson. This is Sun Bird and her son Ghost."

101

Sun Bird smiled and said hello. Charles Pollard looked at her and nodded, and then he picked up Matt and held him as he looked at Judith and said, "We really need to talk Judith. This is no place to raise my grandson."

"Father," Judith said, "Matthew's place is with me and this is where I belong. Maybe when he gets older and can make his own decisions he may decide to attend an Eastern University. If he does I won't try to stop him, I'll support and encourage his decision. If he does decide to attend an Eastern University perhaps that would be your opportunity to support him financially and visit. I think by then he'll be able to deal with your manipulative ways a little better than I did when I was young."

"Manipulative ways?" Charles Pollard asked.

"Yes father," Judith said, "you always interfered with my life and happiness. That's why Matt and I eloped and traveled west to get away from you and your men. We were told that you actually put a contract out on Matt's life, is that true?"

"Of course not Judith, I may be a lot of things but I'm certainly not a killer," Charles Pollard answered.

"I believe you wouldn't have killed him, but I think one of your men would," Judith responded with a hard stare.

"Well," Charles Pollard said, "it looks like your husband got himself killed when he left you and the boy alone at the fort while he traveled west. And then you insult your mother and I by marrying an Indian, what were you thinking Judith?"

"I don't have to explain anything to you father, but if you want to know the truth, I love Storm Warrior. He's a magnificent man, he's smart, educated and one of the highest respected Chiefs among the Sioux. His name is well known by all the tribes, they tell stories of his bravery. He teaches hand-to-hand combat and no one has ever defeated him," Judith answered.

"He sure doesn't look like much," Charles Pollard said as he looked at Storm Warrior standing in front of Many Bears' teepee talking with Gray Horse and Gray Wolf.

"I've never seen an Indian with white hair," Charles Pollard said.

"His white hair happened when he had a vision and was praying. He brought a dead brave back to life, and he has very powerful dreams and visions, he even told me you were coming a week ago," Judith said.

"A week ago?" Charles Pollard said.

"Yes, and apparently three young Shoshone boys were found murdered and the Sioux scouts interpreted smoke signals and read that three white men with two pack animals were traveling west and to advise if you were spotted," Judith said as she glared at him. "Did you and your men murder those boys?"

"No, of course not," Charles answered, "we were attacked, I didn't think about how old they were when they were shooting arrows and us, we shot back and when it was over they were dead."

"The day you shot those boys Storm Warrior was praying and his God showed him that it was you and two other men that had come across the three boys hunting rabbits and you and the others shot those boys and their ponies when they only wanted to greet you. Storm Warrior's God told him it was you and that you would be visiting soon," Judith said as she glared at her father.

"Really, he told you I was coming a week ago?" Charles Pollard said with a surprised look on his face.

"Yes," Judith answered, "we've been expecting you."

"I could use a man of his vision at the bank," Charles Pollard said as he looked towards Storm Warrior, "perhaps you could talk to him for me, I have plenty of room at home for you and the family, and I would pay him well."

"He would never work for you father," Judith said, "he hates you, and he hates what you stand for, he said you murdered those young boys just for fun. And the only reason you and your two men are alive is because you are traveling with the soldiers and the U.S. Deputy Marshals."

"But I have a feeling that when you leave the protection of the fort you'd better take a different route back and travel quickly," Judith said as she glared at him, "there are many looking for the men that murdered those three boys.

"Doesn't it help that I told you they attacked us and we were defending ourselves?" Charles Pollard asked.

"No," Judith answered, "Because I know you are lying."

"You've changed Judith," Charles Pollard said, "you've grown up."

"Yes, I have father," Judith said as she set her jaw and looked at her father, "I've found a new life here. For the first time in my life I'm doing what I choose to do and I've never been happier. Life here is simple, and no one is trying to outwit someone else to steal money or property. There is no crime, everyone respects everyone else. The entire camp watches the children and is covering your back. And every night the campfires are burning and people are visiting. It is a good life here, I've made many friends, and the children that I teach are so polite, they learn fast and absolutely adore me and my husband."

"That all sounds very nice Judith," Charles Pollard said, "but you must return east with me."

"I won't go father," Judith said as she looked him in the eye, "I'm a married woman, I have a child, a husband, and I have a job."

"I don't want to threaten you Judith," Charles Pollard said coldly, "but I'll tell you this, you either come with me or I'll see to it the Sioux nation is devastated, survivors will be rounded up and put on a reservation and Storm Warrior will have a bounty on his head and many will want to collect the reward."

"You do that father," Judith said as her eyes flashed red with rage, "and I will return East, I'll find you and I will shoot you dead wherever I find you."

"Judith," Charles Pollard said with a surprised look on his face, "I'm your father, you would never hurt me."

"You do what you said to the Sioux and you will no longer be my father, I'll be killing a murder of innocent women and children," Judith said angrily.

"I have two men with me that are very good with their pistols, if you don't come back with me there will be a lot of dead Indians and your precious Storm Warrior will be one of them," Charles Pollard said coldly.

"You do that father, and see how long you and your two assassins live," Judith said with fire in her eyes.

"Don't worry Judith," a voice said behind Charles Pollard, "if those two go for their guns I'll shoot them dead."

Charles Pollard turned, Hunt and Earl were standing there and Hunt was lighting a cigarette.

After he lit his cigarette Hunt said, "And after I shoot them I'll put a bullet between your eyes."

"Well Marshall," Charles Pollard said as he turned to face him, "you're mighty sure of yourself."

"Yes," Hunt said, "I am."

Charles Pollard turned towards Judith and said, "Well, I have two-days to stay and visit, perhaps we should continue our visit tomorrow, I need to speak to the Colonel." He handed Matt back to Judith, turned and walked away smiling.

"Marshall," Judith said, "please be careful, I know my father and if he brought some gun hands along they will not give you a chance. They will shoot you in the back if they get a chance."

"Yes, I know their kind well," Hunt said. "But I think they'll behave themselves here and at the fort. But thanks for the concern," Hunt said as he tipped his hat and said, "goodnight Judith."

Judith watched as Hunt, and Earl walked towards Storm Warrior, Gray Horse, Gray Wolf and the Colonel. Then Judith and Sunbird collected the children and walked away to visit a few families sitting around campfires.

Hunt approached the group talking and noticed Charles Pollard talking with the Colonel.

"You know it's only right," Charles Pollard said to the Colonel as Hunt walked up, "that Judith and the boy should go home with me."

"It appears Judith doesn't want to go with you," Lt. Colonel Hawks said in a disgusted voice as he stared at Charles Pollard. "Like she said, she is happy here, and she is married with a child."

"Yes," Charles Pollard said, "a white child, a boy that should be raised back east where he can get a good education."

"She's happy here, the boy is her child, and here is where she's going to stay," the Colonel said, "and I don't want to hear no more about it; understand?"

"Yes, I understand, but you haven't heard the last of it," Charles Pollard said as he turned to walk away.

"Where are you going?" Storm Warrior asked.

Charles Pollard turned and looked at him, "I'm going for a walk if it's any business of yours," he answered.

"You cannot go anyplace without escorts," Storm Warrior reminded him.

"I don't need escorts," Charles Pollard said.

"Yes, you do," Storm Warrior said as he nodded toward four warriors standing nearby. "There are many in the camp aware that you and your men killed those three Shoshone boys and they won't trust you around their children, the warriors are there to protect you from those that may want to take you to the Shoshone. And don't wander away from the main camp, stay where you can be seen and stay away from Judith."

Charles Pollard looked around and knew that wandering around in camp where everyone considered him an enemy could be hazardous.

"Well Storm Warrior," Charles Pollard said, "you make a guest feel real welcome."

"I'm just trying to protect you," Storm Warrior said.

"Fine," he answered, "I'll just stay here and keep you all company. That is if it's OK with you," Charles Pollard said as he walked back to the group as he gave Storm Warrior a hard look.

"How long ago did the two scouts from the fort come to your camp?" Hunt asked as he looked at Gray Horse.

"There were two white traders, and they did not say they were scouts," Gray Horse answered, "here last year when the snow melted. They were rude and wanted to know where they could find the yellow iron that white men call gold. We told them we had no yellow iron and there was none around here. They did not believe us and grew angry, we told them to leave and never come back."

"They left and traveled the trail to the northwest towards the Blackfeet country. We have not seen them since they left," Gray Horse said.

110

"Could you have some of your braves take me to the trail tomorrow and show me the way?" Hunt asked.

"If you wish," Gray Horse said, "I will have some warriors show you the trail, but the men are gone, they have traveled many miles by now."

"Mind if I ride along?" The Colonel asked.

"I thought you had to go tell the troops that we'd be a few days," Hunt said.

"Yes, that's right, I do," the Colonel said. "Will we be traveling out the same way we came?" The Colonel asked as he looked at Gray Horse.

"Yes, we could," Gray Horse answered. "They left by another trail but we can meet the trail after talking to your soldiers."

"Is that OK with you Hunt?" Lt. Colonel Hawks asked.

"Yes, I don't think a few hours will make a difference now," Hunt answered.

"What will you do when you come to the Blackfoot River?" Storm Warrior asked.

"I'm not sure," Hunt answered. "I'd like to talk to the Blackfeet and ask them if they've seen them. The scouts may have visited their camp and perhaps they could tell me what direction they took. Sooner or later I'll find people that remember them. They don't sound like the type that people would forget. I'm sure that if they visited the Blackfeet that the Blackfeet would remember them," Hunt added.

"You got a lot of guts crossing the Blackfoot River," Charles Pollard said. "Aren't they the same ones that attacked and killed everyone in the wagon train?"

"That's a chance I'll have to take," Hunt said. "I met up with some Blackfeet a while back and talked to them. They seemed like a sensible bunch, unlike you and your two traveling companions."

"Why didn't you ask them if they've seen these two army deserters?" Charles Pollard asked.

"I did, they said they haven't seen them but they were posted and looking for three white men that had killed three young Shoshone boys. It seems that the Shoshone and the Blackfeet are friendly. According to what I heard there are Indians posted all over the plains and the mountains looking for you and your two gun hands. I think I'd feel safer traveling alone than with you three," Hunt said.

"Come," Gray Wolf said, "we will walk with you through camp so that all can see you and will know that you are here under our protection. Gray Horse and Storm Warrior, will you walk with me?"

"Yes," they both said and started walking with the four warriors assigned to keep an eye on Charles Pollard following.

They worked their way through camp, stopping to visit, eat boiled or cooked meat and moved on. It was obvious that there were many with cold feelings towards Charles Pollard.

He remained silent as they moved through camp and observed the many cold looks from everyone, including the women. Several camps they visited didn't offer him meat, a sure sign that he was not welcome. However the Colonel, the Captain and the Marshals were warmly greeted.

Teepee's as far as the eye could see were arranged, fires were lit and people were mingling, there was laughter, children were playing, dogs were barking, and men stood in small groups talking. Warriors were dancing around the main lodge fire as drums beat at a steady rythymn. The Colonel and the U.S. Marshals were happy while Charles Pollard acted annoyed.

"Gray Wolf," Storm Warrior said in Sioux, "I feel a need to pray. Please keep an eye on Charles Pollard and keep him away from Judith."

113

"Don't worry Storm Warrior," Gray Wolf said, "he does as I say or I will deliver his body to the Shoshone."

Hunt watched as Storm Warrior disappeared in the crowd and made up his mind to follow him to see what was going on.

Storm Warrior found Sunbird and Judith at Little Bear's teepee. He informed them that he will be praying and not to worry. Then he walked away and walked to a distant hill away from the sound of the camp where he sat quietly as he cleansed his mind and prayed for guidance.

Over an hour passed, Storm Warrior was relaxed both mentally and physically as visions began coming to him accompanied by much lightning and thunder, a sign of much trouble coming like the rain after lightning and thunder.

Visions of Charles Pollard began coming, he was leading a massive invasion of killers, and he was dressed as pictures he had seen of the devil. Truly Charles Pollard was evil and would bring much death and destruction to not only the Sioux, but all plaines Indians would be under his umbrella of death. This will cause the Indians to fight back and this will bring the army. In the end it would bring much death and destruction. Charles Pollard must not be allowed to return east where he would stir much trouble.

It became obvious to Storm Warrior that Charles Pollard must die. His death would save many thousands of lives, not only Indians, but whites as well. Charles Pollard was a man whose life was filled with hatred. He was ruthless, deceitful, and dangerous.

If Charles Pollard had his way Sunbird and Ghost would become a casualty, it became obvious to Storm Warrior what must be done. The vision from Buddha was clear, *Satan has sent a servant in human form and he is walking among you. Satan's messenger must die.*

Chapter 6

Trouble Arrives

S torm Warrior had been at prayer for over an hour, he stood and looked skyward and thanked Buddha for his guidance. As he walked downhill in the dark his mind was on the visions that he had been shown when he sensed someone near.

He stopped and listened with all senses alert for danger. Slowly he withdrew the sword from his back and held it at ready as he stood still and listened. It was then that he smelled the odor of cigarette smoke.

"Marshall Porter," Storm Warrior said, "why are you hiding?"

"I'm not hiding," Hunt answered. "I'm just waiting on you to come back to camp. I don't like to disturb a man when he's praying. How did you know it was me?" Hunt asked.

117

"I could smell you," Storm Warrior answered. "How did you get away from the others?" Storm Warrior asked as he replaced his sword in its sheath.

"It wasn't hard," Hunt said. "With all those people around there was a lot of distractions. I just stepped away and disappeared. I watched you leave and was wondering where you were going, and figured I'd follow," he answered.

"Why were you interested in where I was going?" Storm Warrior asked.

"Well, you talked to Gray Wolf in Sioux, which meant you didn't want us to know what was going on. Let's just say I'm a curious sort of man," Hunt answered as he took a draw on his cigarette.

"Around here your curiosity could get you killed," Storm Warrior said.

"Yes, and I'm curious about something else," Hunt said. "How does a man that is part Chinese come to be a Chief among the Sioux?"

"Ability, integrity and leadership measure men," Storm Warrior answered. "Age does not make a good chief, only knowledge, ability, and integrity. One must prove to be reliable and always be ready to defend the tribe, even unto death if necessary."

118

Hunt-U.S. Marshal III by WL Cox

"That story about finding a skeleton on the riverbank with Chinese moccasins was bogus," Hunt said as he continued, "I know you're the one that everyone was looking for. But relax, as far as I'm concerned the Chinese man everyone was looking for is dead. But tell me; is it true you killed a ship's Co-Captain?"

"Yes, I did," Storm Warrior answered. "He was evil and had beaten a man almost to death, cut his throat, and then threw his body overboard during the trip."

"For my own curiosity, what happened?" Hunt asked.

Storm Warrior told him the story, beginning with the day his parents were murdered and being raised by the Monks. Then he told him about hearing of a ship headed for America and agreed to work on the ship to America in return for a one way trip and how after they were at sea they were made slaves and had to endure long hours and lashes from the guard's whips.

Then he told the story of how when the ship was docked, and the Captain went ashore to sell the goods that he escaped with two others. They separated and went to Philadelphia, and I traveled west.

He told Hunt how after crossing the Missouri river that he was surrounded by what turned out to be Sioux, and he was taken captive. And during the trip back how he ended up fighting Pawnee with the Sioux and how the second night he prayed and a

119

tornado came and how the braves started calling him Storm Warrior and developed a reputation.

"That's quite a story," Hunt said after Storm Warrior finished. "I guess if I were in your shoes I probably would have done the same thing. The bounty on the escaped Chinese man that the bounty hunters had been trying to obtain is gone you know."

"What do you mean?" Storm Warrior asked.

"The Ship left Boston and has never been seen since it sailed, and word is it never made it back to China. It's assumed that the ship sank. With the ship captain gone so is the bounty, and with the report of the Chinese being found dead people quit looking for him. So your secret is safe with me Storm Warrior," Hunt said as they neared the main camp, "let's keep it that way."

"What will become of Charles Pollard?" Storm Warrior asked Hunt.

"I'm not sure," Hunt answered, 'but I think we haven't heard the last of him."

"I think he is filled with evil," Storm Warrior continued, "and he will cause trouble to the Sioux and other Indians on the plaines. He could stir up a war between the whites and the Indians and many will die, both white and Indian."

"And the more trouble, the happier he would be," Hunt added.

120

"Yes, I think you are right," Storm Warrior answered.

"I've noticed," Hunt continued, "that the Sioux doesn't think much of Mr. Pollard."

"No, they do not. They do not respect him; they consider him a dangerous killer, and, they know that he does not like the Sioux," Storm Warrior said.

"I see now why Judith left when she did," Hunt added.

"Yes, I do too," Storm Warrior answered.

Gray Horse joined the group as Storm Warrior, and Hunt walked up.

"We must ride early," Gray Horse said, "I think we should get some sleep."

"Good idea," the Colonel said.

"Come," Gray Wolf said, "we will walk with you to your teepee."

"I'm not quite ready to retire for the evening," Charles Pollard said.

"You don't really have a choice," Hunt said as he nudged him forward.

"Marshall," Charles Pollard said as he turned and gave the Marshall an evil look, "you are beginning to get on my nerves."

121

"Yeah?" Hunt answered, "That makes us even, move it."

Charles Pollard turned and muttered, "Someday soon you will pay" as he started walking.

Hunt did not take Charles Pollard's threat lightly. Hunt knew the man was dangerous and sensed that one day if possible he would hire a killer to fulfill his threat.

A dozen warriors walked up hill with them to the teepee and were left to stand guard after the men entered their guest teepee.

Early the next morning the whites were awakened. They came out of their teepee and were confronted with two thousand warriors mounted and ready to go.

Lt. Colonel Hawks checked his pocket watch. "It's only 4:45 in the morning," he said. Without answering the Sioux brought their horses to them.

"I'm not going on this wild goose hunt," Charles Pollard said as he stared at the waiting warriors.

Storm Warrior rode up to him and said, "That is fine; you will stay in your teepee until we return."

"I will not," Charles Pollard said as he glared up at Storm Warrior.

"If you leave your teepee the guards have orders to kill you," Storm Warrior said as he stared down at him.

"They wouldn't dare," Charles Pollard said indignantly.

"If they don't," Storm Warrior said, "I will kill you when we return."

"Marshal," Charles Pollard said in a stern voice as he glared at Hunt, "you heard the threat, are you going to let them get away with this?"

Hunt mounted his horse and looked down at him. "All I heard was they asking you to please stay in your guarded teepee to protect you. Now if you should stray away from your protected teepee and you happened to end up dead then I'd just write it up that you escaped and we found your body out on the prairie and we buried you where we found you and it appears that you died from dehydration. Yes sir," Hunt said as he turned his head and smiled down at Charles Pollard, "you'd think greenhorns from back east would think to bring along a canteen of water."

"Colonel," Charles Pollard said angrily, "what are you going to do about this?"

"About what?' The Colonel asked. "I didn't hear anything, but the kindness of our guests asking you to stay in your guarded teepee for protection from those that may want to harm you for killing those three Shoshone boys."

"You all will pay for this," Charles Pollard said angrily.

Hunt tipped his hat and said, "You have a nice day Mr. Pollard," as he started to ride away.

"Wait," Charles Pollard shouted. He walked up to his horse and mounted. "I'm going with you."

"Suit yourself," Hunt said as he turned and followed the Colonel out of camp as Gray Horse led the party.

Hunt watched as the twelve Sioux guards mounted their ponies to follow Charles Pollard and watch him carefully, wherever he went they would go.

Charles Pollard caught up to the Colonel, "I'll need my pistol Colonel."

"I think we all would be safer knowing your unloaded pistol is in by saddlebags," the Colonel said evenly without looking at him.

"You don't expect me to ride across the open plains without security do you?" George Pollard argued.

"Nope," the Colonel answered, "the Sioux will protect you."

"You know," Charles Pollard said in a disgusted tone, "when I return don't be surprised if you find yourself demoted and replaced."

124

"That may very well happen," the Colonel said as he looked at Charles Pollard, "with or without your help."

They passed through the narrow canyon and after passing through they rode slowly downhill to where the Sioux guarding the soldiers were camped. The camp had been alerted to their approach, and they were greeted upon arrival.

The Colonel asked permission to speak to his men, and it was granted. Hunt and Earl accompanied Lt. Colonel Hawks to the soldier's camp with George Pollard following.

Hunt waited while the Colonel dismounted and informed the sargent what was going on.

"How are our two guests getting along with the men?" The Colonel asked.

"Not good," the sargent answered. "Those two are asking for trouble. They're the meanest men I've ever met."

"Yeah," the Colonel answered, "and so is Charles Pollard. If he hangs around the Sioux much longer, he'll end up with a few arrows in his sorry ass."

"Maybe you should just turn these three over to the Sioux and let them deal with them," the Captain suggested.

"I've considered it," the Colonel said, "but I'm afraid of any repercussions that could come from it. And besides, some innocents may be killed."

"Yes," the sargent said, "the slender one likes bragging about how fast he is with that pistol and even bragged about killing four men so far, and my men don't like them."

"We have to be going," the Colonel said, "keep a close eye on those two and any sign of trouble I won't be filing any wrongful death charges if one or both end up dead. Captain, I want you to stay here and keep an eye of the men."

"I understand," the Captain answered.

The Colonel remounted and turned to leave when the two bodyguards approached.

'We want to go with Mr. Pollard," Lance Fuller declared.

"You will stay here," the Colonel stated, as they both glared angrily.

"Where's Mr. Pollard," Lance Fuller demanded, "We take orders from him, not you."

"We are on a military mission, and, I am in charge of all military actions in this part of the west. I am in charge, and you will do as I say or you'll be put in irons and you'll stay in irons until we return to the fort, do you understand?" The Colonel asked.

Just as he spoke Hunt and Earl rode up and stopped next to the Colonel.

After the Colonel finished talking Hunt asked, "This man giving you trouble Colonel?"

"Suppose I was," Lance asked, "what would you do about it?"

"Why I guess I'd arrest you and if you went for your gun I'd kill you, that's what I would do," Hunt answered as he glared at Lance.

"You think you're fast enough Marshall?" Lance asked.

"Yep, I sure do," Hunt answered with a smile, "the question is, do you want to do what the Colonel says, or are you willing to die."

"I want to speak to Mr. Pollard," Lance said, "he's the one that pays me and I take orders from him."

Captain Blanchard walked up behind Lance and had his pistol drawn and shoved it into Lance's back. "I'll take your pistol," the Captain said. "I've had enough of your threats, and the men are as sick of it as I am. You'll be in irons until we return to the fort."

Lance was angered; he turned and saw the Captain's pistol shoved into his face and saw that the hammer was pulled back, and his finger was firmly gripping the trigger.

"Go on, go for your gun, I'd love to show the men how your brains look scattered all over the ground," Captain Blanchard said.

Lance looked towards Burt, and many riflemen had rifles leveled at him, so he stood motionless.

"We'll have your pistol also Burt," the Colonel said, "but you won't have to ride back to the fort in irons unless you give us trouble."

The Captain took Lance's pistol from his holster, as one of the soldiers removed the pistol from Burt's holster.

Lance turned and looked at the Colonel, "I thought you said you were in charge, it looks like the Captain is in charge."

"Nope," the Colonel answered with a smile, "he's only following my orders."

"You ordered this?" Lance asked angrily.

"Yes," the Colonel answered, "when the sargent told me about how you threatened my men and kept bragging about how many men you had killed I figured we'd all be a lot safer if you and Burt were unarmed."

"I wasn't causing trouble," Lance argued, "I only wanted to talk to my boss and see what he wanted me to do, is there anything wrong with that?"

"There is when I give you an order and you ignore it," the Colonel answered.

Just then Charles Pollard rode up, "what is going on?" he asked.

"Your gun hands are being relieved of their weapons and Lance here will be placed in irons until we return to the fort," the Colonel answered.

"Why are you doing this to my men?" Charles Pollard asked.

"For refusing to follow my orders," the Colonel said as he looked at him, "and for being a pain in the ass and threatening me and my men. I think we'll all be much safer if they are disarmed."

"Colonel," Charles Pollard said in a heated voice, "when I return home my first priority will be to contact the Secretary of War and file a formal complaint. The army will realize they have the wrong man in charge here when I get through with my story don't be too surprised if you're summoned to Washington to answer charges against you and a man of broader vision is sent to replace you."

"That may very well happen," the Colonel answered, "but while I'm in charge you'll obey my orders and do as I say or you'll join your two traveling companions."

"Colonel," Charles Pollard said, "I think my business is done here. I demand that you allow me, and my men to return to the fort to obtain our packhorses and return home."

Hunt noticed that Chief Gray Horse, Storm Warrior and a dozen other hardened warriors rode up to hear what was being said after watching the soldiers disarm the two gun hands and noticed one was put in irons.

"Mr. Pollard," the Colonel said, "that's some of the best news I've heard come from your mouth since you've arrived."

"Captain," the Colonel said, "I want you and your men to escort Mr. Pollard and his two friends back to the fort. You may return their unloaded weapons to them when they leave the fort, and not before."

"Yes Sir," the Captain said, "but what about you?"

"I plan to travel with Hunt and Earl,' the Colonel answered, "after we follow the missing scout's trail we'll return to the fort."

"Gray Horse," Lt. Colonel Hawks asked, "Could you have some of your warriors escort the soldiers safely to the river?"

Quickly Gray Horse ordered the fifteen hundred warriors that were guarding the soldiers to escort the soldiers. He told Red Elk he was in charge and was to lead them to the river and then return.

As the soldiers prepared to break camp and head south Hunt noticed Gray Horse spoke to several scouts in Sioux. Then suddenly the scouts turned and traveled different directions at a gallop.

"I wonder what he's setting up," Earl asked.

"Well, I'm no genius," Hunt answered, "but from here I'd say he's about to notify the neighborhood about who will be heading east pretty quickly."

Chapter 7

A SKULL IS FOUND

The soldiers, led by Captain Blanchard broke camp and headed south towards the fort with fifteen hundred warriors led by Red Elk.

Hunt, Earl and the Colonel traveled northwest with Gray Horse, Gray Wolf, Storm Warrior and two thousand Sioux warriors to find the trail that the lost white scouts had taken.

It was mid-day when Gray Horse stopped at a stream and shouted an order. Hunt wasn't sure what he had said but judging by how all the warrior's dismounted and began watering their ponies Hunt assumed they were going to rest for a short time.

Hunt noticed Storm Warrior sat his food on a rock and walked up the Coulee and sat on a hill and prayed.

What do you think he's praying for?" Hunt asked Earl.

"I don't know," Earl answered, "except for a Catholic Priest I knew back home, Storm Warrior prays more than any man I've ever known."

When Storm Warrior was finished with his meditation he walked back down the hill just as Gray Horse gave the order to mount up.

Gray Horse had waited until Storm Warrior was finished praying, he learned that sometimes Storm Warrior's prayers and meditation had proved invaluable.

Storm Warrior quickly mounted Wind Fire and joined Gray Horse and Gray Wolf at the head of the party.

Hunt, Earl and the Colonel followed them up the coulee as the trail led them back up onto the plains.

"Tell me," the Colonel said to Hunt, "do you really think you'll be able to find the two missing scouts?"

"If they're alive I'll find them," Hunt answered.

"And if they're dead?" The Colonel asked.

"If they're dead I want to see their graves or their bones. Someone knows what happened to them; I just need to find them," Hunt answered.

"You don't give up do you," the Colonel said as he looked at him.

"I hate unfinished paperwork," Hunt said, "and until I find them or know what happened to them my paperwork will remain unfinished."

"What do you think will happen after Charles Pollard returns home," the Colonel asked?

"He won't return home," Hunt said in a low voice.

"How do you know? The Colonel asked.

"Smoke signals," Hunt answered, "I saw the smoke signals."

"Can you read the smoke signals?" The Colonel asked.

"No, but Gray Horse sent scouts out right after the soldiers headed back to the fort," Hunt said, "and. I think the Sioux alerted the neighboring tribes that the Pollard party will be traveling soon and to be alert. And I think the only reason they're still alive is because of you and the soldiers. The Sioux have no love for those three; I saw the look in their eyes, and I've seen that look many times in my life just before someone died."

The group traveled all day and many times scouts rode in and spoke in Sioux to Gray Horse and then rode off again.

Gray Horse rode back to join Hunt, Earl, and the Colonel. "We are on the same trail that the three whites took as they left our valley," Gray Horse said.

"Will we make camp soon?" The Colonel asked, "we have traveled a great distance today."

"Yes," Gray Horse answered, "ahead is a box canyon with a spring and grass for the ponies. We will camp there."

"Very good," the Colonel said.

After Gray Horse left Hunt looked at the Colonel and spoke.

"Tell me Colonel," Hunt said, "I know you and the Sioux are friendly, but just how much do you really trust them?"

"What do you mean," the Colonel asked.

"If push came to shove, and you got orders to transfer the Sioux and the other plaines tribes to a designated area far from their home how do you think they would respond?" Hunt asked.

"The same way you or I would react should we be told we had to leave the land that our fathers and their fathers have lived since the beginning of time," the Colonel answered. "There would be a war, and many would die."

"Yes, you are right about that," Hunt said, "and it would take a large army to move them."

"I hope to avoid that ever happening," the Colonel said. "I send weekly reports to Washington and report how the Sioux have helped, how they've protected our fort and the men from a number of attacks. That a school has been established on the Sioux land the daughter of a prominent banker from Philadelphia married a Sioux Chief and is teaching the Sioux children how to read and write. I think that the Sioux will set a precedent for the other plains tribes to follow and one-day schools, churches, and retail outlets will be among the lodges and teepees on the Indian land."

"I hope you're right," Hunt said, "but there are too many men that think men like Charles Pollard is right, and your way of thinking is wrong."

"Yes, I know there is some truth in what you say but I hope one day when I'm replaced that the commander in charge of the fort has the vision to see what I see," the Colonel said.

"Yeah, I hope so," Hunt answered, "but don't count on it; I don't have a lot of confidence in the army, no disrespect aimed at you Colonel."

Several hours passed and just as the sun was starting to set in the west the party led by Gray Horse arrived at the boxed canyon. Wolves were posted, and scouts were sent out.

"The missing men surely would have camped here," Gray Horse said to Hunt. "Here they would be protected from the wind; they would have grass and water for their ponies, and there is only one way in."

"Yes, I think you're right," Hunt said as he looked around and remembered what the Blackfoot warrior Bull had told him.

"I think I'll scout around those rocks," Hunt said, "If they were attacked here they would have taken refuge and fired from behind those rocks."

Hunt and Earl walked uphill to the rocks and began looking around as Gray Horse returned to his men and ordered them to set up camp.

Gray Horse ordered scouts posted at different spots throughout the canyon as he gazed up at Hunt and Earl searching the area behind the rocks carefully for sign.

After looking around Hunt, and Earl came back down to the fire and sat on a log near the fire.

"Something just doesn't add up," Hunt said to the Colonel, "these two had a reputation for causing trouble. But after leaving the Sioux camp they vanished from the face of the planet."

"Maybe they went up to Canada," the Colonel said.

"Yeah maybe," Hunt said, "but I'm sure that wherever they went word would have gotten to us about any trouble that they may have caused, and I haven't heard anything."

"What do you think happened to them?" The Colonel asked.

"I have a feeling," Hunt said, "that they visited the Sioux, and I don't know what happened but with your scout's reputation I'm sure they managed to rub the Sioux the wrong way and I don't think they lived too long after they left."

"You're thinking the Sioux killed them?" The Colonel asked.

"If the men insulted them, or threatened them, yes I do," Hunt answered. "I've watched the Sioux closely; they're very big on respect and following orders. Although I've never seen your Storm Warrior in action, I have a feeling he can handle himself quite easily."

"Colonel," Hunt said as he narrowed his eyes and looked at him, "you know as well as I do who Storm Warrior actually is. Suppose those two scouts came here looking for him and to protect him the Sioux did away with them."

The Colonel looked at Hunt and thought before answering. "You know who Storm Warrior is and where he came from?" The Colonel asked.

"Of course I do, and when I was talking to some of the soldiers they told me that the scouts bragged about the reward they were going to collect when they found him and hauled him back to Boston," Hunt said.

"I talked to Storm Warrior back at the Sioux camp last night," Hunt said. "He knows that I know, and I told him it would stay silent with me. I'll never tell anyone. But you know, don't you Colonel."

"Yes," the Colonel admitted, "I've suspected for a long time, but I've never said anything to him. He's been a good friend and has saved many of my men's lives in battle, including Captain Blanchard's. I've grown to respect him, and I think he is a good man."

"Yes, I think he is too," Hunt added. "But I also think he knows what happened to your missing scouts."

"You could be right," the Colonel answered as he thought about it for a moment, "but if you do find the men alive I think they'd be taken back and hung for the murder of the Robinson family and the rape of Mrs. Robinson and their two daughters. One girl was only twelve years old, and the other was fourteen. I'd sure like to get my hands on those two, and if we find out the Sioux did kill them then I'd feel like they deserved it."

"There's no doubt that they asked for it," Hunt added, "I'd just like to know where they are buried so I can urinate on their graves and get a lot of paperwork off my desk. And if they threatened the Sioux or raped one of their women I wouldn't hold any bad feelings towards them if they did kill them."

A warrior rode up and spoke to Gray Horse. Gray Horse turned and looked towards the Colonel and Hunt then he walked over to them.

"My scout found a skull," Gray Horse reported, "it could be one of the men you are looking for."

"What makes you think it's one of the men I'm looking for," Hunt asked.

"The skull has a gold tooth," Gray Horse said.

"Say," the Colonel said, "Matt Collins, the big man with a scar on his face, he had a gold tooth."

"Why don't you come with us," Hunt said, "you could identify the location of the gold tooth in his mouth."

The Colonel, Hunt, Earl and a dozen Sioux all walked to where the scout found the skull. He pointed downhill to a depression in the ground where a skull was lying on its side and was mostly covered in sand and dirt. The gold tooth was exposed, and as the sun set the tooth reflected a glimmer of light.

The Colonel and the Marshal's walked down to where the skull was and picked it up.

"Yes," Lt. Colonel Hawks said as he examined the skull, "that's the exact location of Matt Collin's gold tooth, and this must be what's left of him."

141

Hunt knelt down on his knees and dug around in the ground with his hands and soon started finding more bones. As he uncovered more bones, he found an Army rifle and a gun belt. The rifle had been fired.

Hunt handed the items to the Colonel and continued digging in a little wider circle. Then he discovered an arrow.

Hunt examined the arrow and looked up at Gray Horse and asked, "Is this a Sioux arrow?

"That is a Blackfoot arrow," Gray Horse answered as he stared down at him.

"I'll take your word for it," Hunt said as he handed the arrow to the Colonel.

"There were two men," Hunt said, "it appears there's only one body here.

Are you sure that the golden tooth belongs to the man known as Matt Collins?" Earl asked.

"Yes," the Colonel answered, "it's the same tooth."

"Did he ever say where he had the gold tooth done?" Hunt asked.

"No, he used to brag about it and he used to polish it to show it off," Lt. Colonel Hawks answered. "His paperwork said he was from Virginia, I'd say he probably did it in Virginia."

142

Hunt put the skull, the three bones and the arrow he found in a cloth sack and hung it from his saddle horn. Using a stick, he scraped around on the ground for sign of more bones.

"It only makes sense," Earl said, "that the other man should be here too."

"Yes, it does," the Colonel answered. "Of course wild animals could have dragged the body off."

"Yes, that's a possibility," Hunt answered, "but let's assume they were here when they were attacked. I think we should check behind the rocks up there, if they were attacked I'm sure they would have taken refuge and fired from behind the rocks."

"We could find shell casings, an article of clothing, or bones," Hunt said.

"OK," the Colonel said, "maybe we should ask Gray Horse if some of his warriors could help us search, they have sharp eyes and are used to looking for sign."

"Let us look first," Hunt said as he started climbing the hill and began searching the ground.

Earl and the Colonel climbed a different spot to avoid covering the same ground. After thirty minutes, the shadows from the setting sun were making it difficult to see, so they called off the search.

"Do you suppose," the Colonel asked as they climbed down to the ground, "that it's likely the other one may have shot him?"

"Anything is possible at this point," Hunt said as he followed the Colonel down to level ground, "but why would his own partner shoot him?"

"The two missing men traveled together, but I wouldn't call them friends," the Colonel answered. "He thought Matt Collins was a troublemaker and talked too much. I often heard him telling Matt to shut his mouth, or keep quiet."

"Well," Hunt said, "in the morning we'll search for more sign, but for now I think we should join the Sioux at the fire and get something to eat."

As they walked towards the fire, Hunt spoke to Lt. Colonel Hawks.

"Let's suppose," Hunt said, "that Matt Collins figured out that Storm Warrior was actually the Chinese runaway that had a thousand dollar bounty on his head, but with over five thousand Sioux he knew he'd need help."

"And let's assume those two camped here or took refuge after leaving the Sioux camp and the Sioux decided to kill them to keep them silent," Hunt added."

"That's quite an assumption," the Colonel said. "Remember, we found what Gray Horse said was a Blackfoot arrow with the body."

"Yes," Hunt answered, "it wouldn't take any effort to plant an arrow. I'm sure with all the battles between the Sioux and Blackfeet there would have been a lot of Blackfeet arrows lying around to be picked up and planted."

"I see what you mean," the .Colonel answered.

"And let's say you are right," Lt. Colonel Hawks answered, "these two were the scum of the earth, if what you say is right then I think they saved us from a trial and a hanging."

"Isn't it enough to know that they are dead and let it go?" Lt. Colonel Hawks asked.

"I wished it were that easy," Hunt answered. "I need to put the details of their deaths together, and I need to know if the other one is dead."

As Hunt, Earl and the Colonel reached the campfire, Hunt looked around and asked, "Where is Storm Warrior?"

Gray Wolf pointed up the hill, and Storm Warrior's form could be made out as he knelt in prayer.

"I see," Hunt said as he sat down.

"He prays a lot, doesn't he," the Colonel said as he gazed up the hill at Storm Warrior.

"Yes," Gray Horse said, "he says he asks for guidance, advice and sometimes he sees things to come, or calls upon a great storm to stop the enemy."

"Have you found his guidance from prayer useful?" the Colonel asked?

"Yes, many times," Gray Horse answered as he chewed a piece of meat.

"So what did his God say to him about Judith's father?" Hunt asked.

"Six suns before Charles Pollard arrived, Storm Warrior told of a man from the east was traveling and that he was a very dangerous man and would cause death and suffering to the Sioux. He also said that he and his men were killing Indians that they met and that they were even killing children. His God told him that the men would be surrounded by warriors on their return and would be captured, and would suffer a painful death for killing the children. I told Storm Warrior we should kill them but he said no, that the revenge should be for the Shoshone," Gray Horse said as he continued eating.

"After meeting these men, I saw evil, and I do not think you, or the Colonel liked them either," Gray Horse said.

146

"Well Gray Horse, you're right," the Colonel answered, "there's not many whites that like him and I think many have tried to kill him in the past but with the help of his two gun hands that escort him everywhere he goes they haven't been very successful. And if the Shoshone try to take them I think many Shoshone will die."

"Maybe," Gray Horse said, "but I think they'll find killing skilled warriors will be a little more difficult than killing curious children that ride up to them to visit or trade."

"Is that why you had your braves send signals to the Pawnee and Shoshone that they would be leaving the fort soon?" Hunt asked as he looked up at Gray Horse.

"If the Shoshone and Pawnee watched them return to the fort," Gray Horse said, "they would think that the soldiers were protecting them."

"They could become angry and attack the fort and kill all the soldiers to get the men that killed their young. I did not think that you wanted that to happen," Gray Horse said as he glared into Hunt's eyes.

"Is that what you would do?" Hunt asked.

Gray Horse threw the bone into the fire that he was eating on, and gave Hunt a deadly serious look as he said, "if they had killed Sioux children they would never have made it to the fort."

147

"You would have killed them?" Hunt asked.

"If they had killed your children, what would you have done?" Gray Horse asked.

"I would have hunted them down and shot them," Hunt answered.

"You would have treated them better than the Sioux would have," Gray Horse said as he cut off another piece of meat and began chewing on it.

"What would you have done?" Hunt asked.

"They would have died a slow and painful death," Gray Horse said as he looked at Hunt.

"Well," Hunt said, "I wouldn't blame you. And quite honestly, I don't blame you for tipping off the Pawnee and the Shoshone. But they may take a different trail when they return."

"Yes," Gray Horse said, "if I were them, I know that I would take a different trail."

"What if they return to your camp to take Judith and her son with them, what would you do?" Hunt asked.

"I do not think they would be so stupid," Gray Horse answered.

"I wouldn't be so sure," Hunt said. "They may think the Sioux would be friendlier than your neighbors and try to get back to your camp for safety and take Judith at gunpoint."

"If they return they will be ordered to leave," Gray Horse said as he bit off a piece of meat, "they would not be welcomed and they would not be allowed to return to the camp."

"Charles Pollard can be very persuasive," Hunt said as he bit off a piece of meat.

"So can I," Gray Horse answered coolly.

"Hunt," the Colonel said as the two men stared at each other, "you and I both know how belligerent Charles Pollard can be. If he and his men returned to the Sioux land and they ended up dead it would become my responsibility to investigate, and my article will read that the Sioux acted in self-defense."

Hunt turned and looked at the Colonel and said, "and then you'd better make sure your report is complete and accurate. Washington will have a lot of questions; I wouldn't want them to find any discrepancies and call you back to Washington to explain."

"A point well taken," the Colonel answered, "and you can bet your life any statement coming from me will be complete and accurate."

149

"Gray Horse," Hunt asked, "you are a man of many battles and wisdom, why do you think we only found the remains of one man and not two?"

"I don't know," Gray Horse answered as he looked at Hunt, "maybe only one man died here."

"Maybe," Hunt said as he bit off another piece of meat, "but in the morning I'd like the support of your warriors to search the entire canyon looking for more bones, rifle shell casings, clothing, or any sign of the missing man."

Gray Horse nodded, "in the morning," he said, "I will have my warriors once again search the ground and the boulders for any sign of your lost man. If he died here, we should find some sign."

"Thank you," Hunt said, "I do appreciate your support."

Then there was a voice behind Hunt, it was Storm Warrior. "Your men died here," he said as he stepped into the light of the fire and sat next to Gray Wolf. "Buddha has shown me that there was a conflict, and they are dead. Coyotes have scattered their bones; you will not find them here."

"Did Buddha tell you who killed them?" Hunt asked as he looked at Storm Warrior suspiciously.

"Warriors were camped here, they were traveling and not from around here. The men spotted them; there were only a few, others saw them coming, and remained hidden in the rocks to see

150

their intentions, they said they came to trade; they tried to cheat the warriors and insulted them, and then there was a battle. When it was over the traders were dead."

"And did your Buddha show you who the Indians were or where they were from?" Hunt asked.

"No," Storm Warrior answered, "he only showed me that they were evil and that they deserved to die."

"Yes," Hunt answered rolled a cigarette, "they weren't exactly model citizens. If I had found them alive I'd arrest them and they would stand trial for murder, and, rape, and, they would have hung. But I just can't write in my report that unknown Indians on Sioux land killed them, especially when the Sioux have scouts covering their entire nation and know every time someone crosses into their land."

"Many times," Gray Horse said, "warriors from other tribes cross Sioux land and manage to remain out of sight. There are many valleys, hills, trees and rocks to hide. Sometimes they travel at night to avoid being seen, and many times we have found tracks, but, never saw the ones that made them."

"I see your point," Hunt said, "I guess it's possible, but I would suspect they wouldn't stay around long. We found a Blackfoot arrow near the skull with a gold tooth. Do you think it's likely that the Blackfeet are responsible?"

151

"It's possible," the Colonel said as he spoke up, "it was the Blackfeet that attacked the wagon train."

"Whoever killed these two," Storm Warrior said as he spoke up, "killed evil men that deserved to die. Even the whites wanted them dead, and they made no friends among the tribes. If they had not died here others would be murdered, robbed and raped, perhaps that is what you should write in your report."

"Yes," Hunt said as he drew a last puff off of his rolled cigarette and put it out, "maybe I will write that in my report along with the name of the tribe that killed them."

"Washington is funny, they want details," Hunt added, "and when details are missing more men show up to find the answers, especially when the missing men are government or military men.

"We will search the canyon in the morning," Gray Horse said, "If he died here we should find a sign. If we find no sign then perhaps he rode away."

"Yes," Hunt said, "or were taken away, we will search tomorrow. I'm going to turn in for the night."

"Me too," the Colonel said as he stood.

After Hunt, Earl and the Colonel bedded down Gray Horse spoke in Sioux to Storm Warrior and Gray Wolf. "This could cause trouble to the Sioux if the other body is found on Sioux land."

"They were evil men," Gray Wolf said, "I cannot understand why the Marshals need to understand why and how they died.'

"It would be the same if Sioux warriors had died," Storm Warrior said, "we would want to know how they died and track down the killers."

"Yes," Gray Wolf said, "but we would have been much quicker at it."

"I feel bad," Storm Warrior said, "about not telling the truth about what happened to these men. We did not know that they were working for the fort, we thought they were evil traders."

"They were evil traders," Gray Wolf said, "they never told us they worked as scouts for the fort. All they wanted was to kill you and take you back for a reward."

"Yes," Gray Horse said, "they were evil men and today people are alive because they are dead. They needed to die; I am glad we killed them."

"What do you think the Marshals would do if we told him the truth about what happened to them?" Storm Warrior asked.

"The man named Hunt appears to be a man that doesn't believe what he hears," Gray Horse said as Gray Wolf nodded agreement, "and besides that, he would know who you are and where you came from," he added.

"He already knows who I am and where I came from," Storm Warrior told them. "Back at the camp after the council meeting I went to pray and when I came down from the hill he was waiting for me. He told me he knows who I am, and he asked me the story. I told him, and, he told me he would not tell and that he didn't blame me, he said he would have done the same."

"Hunt is very smart, if he were a Sioux he would make a Great War Chief," Gray Horse said, "and he seems to be a fair man. I will think about it tonight, maybe tomorrow I will tell the truth about what happened to those evil men."

"Yes,' Storm Warrior said, "they were ready to kill me and take Wind Fire and go to a place called New Orleans. They were saying how much money they could get for bringing my body back and how much they could sell Wind Fire for and the good time they could have in New Orleans after collecting the bounty and selling Wind Fire."

"The truth is always best," Storm Warrior said as he looked at Gray Horse and Gray Wolf.

"And what if he wants to take you back with him to stand a white man's trial for killing the soldier's scouts?" Gray Wolf asked.

"I did not kill them," Storm Warrior said, "I was alone, and, they were pointing a gun at me. I do not know who fired the

154

arrows that killed them. He cannot arrest all the warriors and I don't think he would be stupid enough to try."

"No," Gray Horse answered, "but one day he could return with many soldiers to avenge the deaths of the three army scouts, and many would die."

"I do not think," Storm Warrior said thoughtfully, "that the evil men's deaths would be avenged. I guess," He continued, "that the whites would be grateful knowing that they no longer have to search for them and that they met a justified end."

"I will wait," Gray Horse said, "and we will see what happens if the other man's bones are found tomorrow."

Coyotes could be heard from the hills around them, and Gray Horse looked up towards where the sound came from.

"Coyotes," Gray Horse said, "have separated the bones and may have drug their bodies into the hills. We will search until the sun is high then I will order my warriors to return, and, we will leave."

"What if the Marshals won't leave," Gray Wolf asked?

"Then we will leave without them and they will be on their own," Gray Horse answered.

"What about the Colonel?" Storm Warrior asked.

"He will travel with us," Gray Horse said, "I do not think he would wait, he has duties at the fort and men depend on him."

Hunt talked quietly to Colonel Hawks. "I wish I understood the Sioux language," he said, "I'd like to know what they're talking about."

"I suspect," the Colonel said as he looked towards the group, "they are talking about the bones they found today of Matt Collins."

"I'll bet they know exactly what happened to both of them," Hunt said under his breath, "and I have a feeling we're traveling with the individuals responsible for their demise."

"That may be so," the Colonel said, "and if the Sioux are responsible, I'll bet the two somehow threatened or insulted them, they set a trap and the two idiots walked into it."

"If a trap were set," Hunt added, "I'd say the word came down from the council and the three sitting around the campfire talking carried it out with a little help from a couple thousand warriors."

"Good night Hunt," The Colonel said as he closed his eyes.

Chapter 8

WHERE ARE THE SCOUTS

E arly the following morning all gathered around the fire and ate. Gray Horse approached the Marshals, "we will search the canyon and the rocks above. When the sun is high, we will head back."

"And what if we don't find anything?" Hunt asked.

"Then they will not be here," Gray Horse answered as he ate.

"Why can't we wait until we find them?" Hunt asked suspiciously.

"We are near the Blackfoot River," Gray Horse explained, "scouts have reported Blackfeet watching our camp, they know we are here. If we wait too long the Blackfeet could mount an attack and many would die."

Hunt thought about what Gray Horse had just told him and sighed. "OK," he said, "till noon."

The eastern sky was glowing light as it began filtering through the light fog and began illuminating the ground.

"It will be light enough to see soon," Gray Horse said, "I will have my warriors begin searching," as he stood and left to tell the warriors what he wanted them to do.

Gray Horse returned to the fire, "a thousand warriors will search, the rest are to remain on guard as the Blackfeet are organizing a large group of warriors on the other side of the river, and the river lie's only a-mile from the valley. I have sent scouts to watch our flanks," he explained, "a large group of warriors could have crossed the river at night and the Blackfeet could attack from several sides, and if they planned it right they could divide our forces."

Hunt began respecting Gray Horse's savvy.

"Why would they attack?" Hunt asked, "I thought they were at peace with the Sioux."

"Yes," Gray Horse said, "we have talked of peace, but when the Blackfeet sees a large party of Sioux close to their land they could think we are preparing to attack. Scouts have reported that more Blackfeet are arriving, and their numbers are greatly increasing. They may grow weary of waiting and decide to attack when their numbers increase. The Blackfeet's words cannot be trusted. Many have died during times of peace when one has an advantage over another."

"I see," Hunt said as he thought. "Why can't you just send a rider over with a white flag and tell them that you have no plans to attack and that we are only searching for the two white scouts that disappeared last spring?"

"We have had many battles over the years with the Blackfeet," Gray Horse explained, "there are many that have lost members of their family and they may be looking for a way to avenge their death. It has always been this way; it is better not to trust the Blackfeet."

"What will happen if they attack?" Hunt asked. "We will fight from the rocks," Gray Horse said, "they would lose many if they are foolish enough to attack.

"Well," Hunt said, "let's get started looking for sign of the other two men."

Hunt, Earl and the Colonel walked with Gray Horse as Storm Warrior and Gray Wolf followed.

Gray Horse ordered one of the scouts to send smoke signals for more warriors in case the Blackfeet did decide to attack.

Gray Horse quickly organized his warriors and sent them different directions to search the ground and rocks above.

"We only have a few hours," Gray Horse said, "and then we must leave."

Hunt watched the warriors scratching the ground with sticks, lances and bows as he sighed and said, "Well, if we don't find anything within a few hours I don't think we will find any sign of them. I want to thank you for your help Gray Horse," Hunt said.

***

The Blackfeet were organizing quite a large group of warriors. White Hawk, an older chief with the Blackfeet heard of the gathering and rode with twenty warriors out to the area where the warriors were gathered near the river.

White Hawk knew that a young war chief by the name of Spotted Elk was leading the raiding party and White Hawk rode out to convince him to call off the attack.

Most of the three thousand warriors gathered were younger and inexperienced in the ways of war. The Sioux were a powerful foe and to have so many young and inexperienced warriors would mean that many Blackfeet would die.

160

White Hawk found Spotted Elk, "Do not attack, do not cross the river." he said.

Spotted Elk laughed, "If White Hawk is afraid of the mighty Sioux then perhaps he should return to the camp with the women and children."

"Spotted Elk," White Hawk said as he stared fiercely into his eyes, "do you know how many Sioux you will be facing?"

"Scouts have told me that there are no more than five hundred Sioux," Spotted Elk said confidently, "and my scouts say that Storm Warrior and Gray Horse are leading," he stated as he stared back at White Hawk, "we can strike a mighty blow to the Sioux by killing these Sioux."

"I have been in many battles with the Sioux," White Hawk said, "chiefs like the Gray Horse and Storm Warrior do not travel this far from camp with only five hundred warriors. I say there are no less than two thousand warriors, and if you cross the river to attack you will find yourself in a trap, and you will lose many warriors."

"A trap?" Spotted Elk scoffed. "We are over three thousand strong, and our numbers are growing, many are anxious to test their medicine against the Sioux; if we attack, many Sioux will die."

"If you attack," White Hawk said, "many Blackfeet will die and if you live you will find yourself running for the river before the battle is over. Don't allow yourself to be drawn into an attack when you don't even know for sure how many you will be facing or where the central force is located."

"They are trapped in the Boxed Canyon," Spotted Elk answered

"Do not attack," White Hawk said as he glared into Spotted Elk's eyes, "many warriors have died in battle with the Sioux when they attacked without knowing how many Sioux they were facing and where their forces were located."

"Look around you," White Hawk said. "You don't see many older and experienced warriors because most have died in combat. Most of our warriors are inexperienced. The only taste of action has been burying the dead. You are young, and you have never led warriors into battle. War Chiefs before you have died in battles, who will be chosen for War Chief after a Sioux takes your scalp?"

"The sign of a great Chief is to act cautiously, display wisdom and plan an attack after scouts have provided numbers and locations."

"My scouts have given me numbers," Spotted Elk answered, "and they are camped in the boxed canyon."

"The boxed canyon, of course," White Elk said as he thought to himself, "it is a trap, there will be Sioux warriors in the rocks above, and you will lose many warriors if you are stupid enough to ride your warriors into the trap. Be smart, Spotted Elk, send a brave over to talk to the scouts and ask to speak to Gray Horse. When the Sioux scout takes the scout to talk to Gray Horse you find out where they are located and why they are there."

Spotted Elk thought about the words of the older and wiser White Elk.

"I need a volunteer to ride over and talk to the Sioux Scouts," Spotted Elk announced.

Finally, a young warrior volunteered.

"No," White Elk said to Spotted Elk, "he is too young, you need to send an older and wiser warrior."

"Why must we waste time," the young brave that volunteered asked. "We are a powerful force, we can attack and destroy all the Sioux."

"You see," White Elk said to Spotted Elk, "if you act on the words of the young and stupid you will be as they are, young and stupid."

"I will go myself," White Elk said, "I will ask to speak to Gray Horse; I will see their camp and I will see their numbers."

163

"And what if they kill you and take your scalp?" Spotted Elk asked.

"The Sioux will not kill someone coming to speak, we are at peace with the Sioux, and they have never broken a peace unless they are attacked. You must keep your braves on this side of the river until I return," Chief White Elk demanded.

"I will keep my warriors here," Spotted Elk said, "but if you do not return we will attack."

"I will return before the sun sets in the west," White Elk answered, "do not attack."

Then White Elk turned his pony and entered the water and carefully walked his pony across the river and galloped up the hill towards the Sioux scouts.

When he reached the top of the hill he raised his right hand as a sign of peace and stopped.

"My name is White Elk," a chief with the Blackfeet. "I wish to speak to Gray Horse."

***

Hunt, Earl, and the Colonel were searching the rocks for any sign of the missing man when Hunt noticed a warrior galloping his pony inside the boxed canyon and spoke to Gray Horse, Gray Wolf and Storm Warrior.

"Something is up," Hunt said to Earl and the Colonel as they walked down to find out what the scout had to say.

"What's up?" Hunt asked as he approached.

"There is a Blackfoot chief by the name of White Elk that wants to talk," Gray Horse answered.

"I want to ride out with you," Hunt said, "He may know something about the man we're searching for."

Hunt, Earl, Lt. Colonel Hawks, Gray Horse, Gray Wolf, Storm Warrior and twenty warriors rode out to see what the Blackfoot chief had to say.

Soon a number of Sioux were riding out to where he waited, and White Elk was surprised to see the Colonel from the fort and two white men with a star on their shirts riding with Gray Horse, Gray Wolf and Storm Warrior accompanied by twenty warriors.

He was not aware that Gray Horse had ordered his men to hide in the rocks above and to not show themselves if they rode back into the boxed canyon.

As the Sioux drew close he saw for the first time the face of Gray Horse, Gray Wolf and Storm Warrior.

"I am Gray Horse," he said, "you asked to speak to me?"

"I am White Elk, a chief with the Blackfeet, why do you bring so many warriors close to Blackfeet land?" He asked.

"We are on Sioux land," Gray Horse answered.

"My scouts think you are a war party and will attack the Blackfeet," White Elk said.

"We will not attack the Blackfeet," Gray Horse answered, "we are at peace."

"Why are you here?" White Elk asked.

Gray Horse looked at him and didn't think he should explain to a Blackfoot what he was doing on his own land. However, he quickly thought, he had the courage to ride across the river alone and ask to speak to a Sioux War Chief.

Gray Horse pointed to the white men with a star on their shirts, "their names are Hunt and Earl, "they are searching for two white scouts that have disappeared. No one has seen them since they left the white man's fort last year after the snow melted."

White Elk looked at the Marshals, "who is the soldier?"

166

"This is Lt. Colonel Hawks from the Fort," Gray Horse answered, "he is helping the Marshals find his missing scouts."

Hunt rode his horse forward a few steps, "White Elk, have you seen the missing scouts, they sometimes identify themselves as traders, one was a large man with a scar across his face," he said.

White Elk eyed the Marshal and knew at a glance that he was a man of courage and was heavily armed. His lean muscular features were covered in dark skin from the sun and wind.

"Two winters ago," White Elk answered in English, white men came to our camp and asked many questions. They wanted to know where the white man's gold was and then asked questions about a Chinese man. It is said he was short and had slanted eyes, we told him we had never seen such a man, they grew angry and left. They did not say they were scouts or traders. One man had a scar across his face and he was large."

"They left our land and traveled south; we have never seen them again," Chief White Elk said.

"Is it possible that some of your braves followed them and attacked and killed them?" Hunt asked.

"It is possible," White Elk said, "but the braves would have taken their ponies and weapons, I have not seen any of these among our tribe. They came in peace, so we let them leave in peace."

167

"What trail did they take when they left your village?" Hunt asked.

"They traveled south," White Elk answered, "Perhaps they took the trail to visit the Cheyenne, or maybe they returned to the fort."

"Thank you," Hunt said as he placed his fingers on the front of his hat and tipped it in a polite gesture.

Then White Elk looked at Gray Horse, "How many warriors are you traveling with."

"Enough," Gray Horse answered.

"When two thousand Sioux come close to the Blackfeet land it makes our people nervous and they mount a large war party to protect our people," White Elk said, "we do not gather to attack, only to protect our land."

"You can order your warriors back to camp," Gray Horse said, "we do not plan to attack or cross the Blackfoot River. But if we are attacked we will defend our land and our people. We have given the Blackfeet permission to hunt the buffalo that crosses the Sioux land. When the hunters come we only observe, we do not attack. All tribes must eat and collect hides for their teepees. It is to honor our word to the Blackfeet that we allow this. If the Blackfeet attack or show aggression against the Sioux the Blackfeet will no longer be allowed to hunt the Buffalo on Sioux land."

"It is good," White Elk said, "that two chiefs of different tribes meet in peace and talk. No one likes burying their sons that die in combat."

"Yes," Gray Horse said, "it is good, but peace can only be maintained when one's spoken words are kept.'

White Elk raised his hand as a sign of peace, "I will return now and tell my warriors to stay on their side of the river. It is good that no one dies today."

"Yes, talking is better than dying," Gray Horse said as he returned the raised hand peace sign.

White Elk turned his pony and rode away at a slow gallop with the two scouts riding with him.

As they disappeared over the hill, the Colonel said, " I think that went well."

"He is not a war chief," Gray Horse said, "he must return to convince the war chief and his braves to return to their village without attacking. If he fails they will attack, I do not trust the Blackfeet words."

Gray Horse led the way as they rode back to the canyon as White Elk and the two scouts reached the top of the hill overlooking the river. The two scouts stopped and watched as White Elk rode down the grassy hill and crossed the river to rejoin the Blackfeet.

169

Gray Horse arrived back at camp within the boundaries of the dead end canyon, and everyone dismounted. Gray Horse gave the order to resume the search and one of the warriors came up and told Gray Horse and spoke in Sioux that he found another skeleton.

Gray Horse turned and looked at the Marshals, "my warriors have found more bones."

"Where?" Hunt asked.

Gray Horse asked him to show them the bones and everyone followed the warrior up hill and pointed to the ground behind a rock.

Hunt dug in the ground around the exposed bone and found a partial rib cage attached to a vertebra.

"Not much to go by," the Colonel said as he looked at the bones uncovered by Hunt.

After extensive searching of the earth no more bones were found.

"Coyotes drug the body here," Gray Horse said, "Coyotes fight over the carcass, they pull the body apart and carry parts away to eat, many bones get eaten, others are scattered.'

"Do you think," Hunt asked looking at Gray Horse, "both men died here?"

170

"Yes," Gray Horse said. "The rib cage is too small for the large man with a gold tooth."

"What do you think happened to them?" The Marshall asked.

"The Blackfeet guard this part of the river closely because it is low enough for a pony to cross. The Blackfeet may have spotted the white men and formed a raid, or the white men may have caused trouble and ran here for cover," Gray Horse answered.

"Marshal," the Colonel said, "my report will read that there is enough evidence to indicate the scouts engaged in a battle with the Blackfeet and died here."

"My report," Hunt said as he looked at the Colonel, "will say they were killed by Indians, One Blackfoot arrow is not enough evidence to blame the Blackfeet for their demise. Let's continue searching and see if we can find anything else before we head back."

Gray Horse gave the word and the warriors resumed their search along with the Colonel, Hunt and Earl.

Twenty minutes later one of the warriors let out a war hoop sound and everyone looked up. He held his lance high and waited as Hunt, Earl, Lt. Colonel Hawks, Gray Horse and Storm Warrior climbed up to where the warrior waited while others gathered to see what was found.

171

It was another skull. Hunt began digging and uncovered a number of bones.

"This arm bone shows sign of being hit either by an arrow or a bullet," Hunt said.

"The sun is high," Gray Horse said, "we must leave."

"First we need to bury the remains and mark their graves," Hunt answered.

Hunt and Earl dug two shallow graves and marked each grave with a stick. After covering the bones, they were ready to leave.

Chapter 9

The Challenge

H unt made notes in his book and wrote down the location of the graves and the area in the canyon where the bones were found. Hunt added a rough sketch of the valley and where the Blackfoot River was located.

Hunt noted that the cause of death was believed to be Indians and no particular tribe was noted, although a Blackfoot arrow was found near the remains of Burt Hanson and the remains were found on Sioux land with the help of Sioux Warriors.

A scout rode in and reported to Gray Horse that Running Calf of the Northern Sioux was approaching with twenty five hundred warriors; other scouts rode in, and most reported all was quiet but the scout from the Blackfoot River reported that the warriors on the other side of the river were acting anxious to attack. There were shouts of insults and warriors were riding their

173

ponies back and forth challenging the Sioux scouts to come to the river.

"Watch them," Gray Horse said, "if they cross the river ride your ponies back to the canyon."

The scout returned to watch the river and Gray Horse, Storm Warrior and Gray Wolf gathered together to talk.

"What's going on," Hunt asked Lt. Colonel Hawks.

"I don't know," the Colonel answered, "scouts keep coming in and talking to Gray Horse then ride out again, and Gray Horse is acting concerned about something."

"I thought Gray Horse was anxious to ride out at high noon," Hunt said. "It's past 1:00 in the afternoon; I wonder what's holding him up?"

"I'm sure he has a good reason," the Colonel answered. "I've never seen him make a mistake on the trail."

"I would think with the large group of Blackfeet at the river that he would want to get going very soon and put distance between himself and the Blackfeet," Earl said.

"I'm not so sure that would be a smart move," the Colonel said. "If they catch up with us out in the open we'll be outnumbered three to one. If they attack us here we will have a lot of cover and the Blackfeet would lose many warriors. It could be that the Blackfeet are waiting for us to leave the protection of the canyon, then send some scouts across the river to get an idea how many Sioux are in the group and attack."

Gray Horse ordered signals to be sent that they were waiting at the Canyon and that over three thousand Blackfeet were organized on the other side of the river and were threatening to attack. A short time later the signals were sent and from five miles away Running Calf read the message. He estimated that it would take him less than an hour to reach the canyon, and Gray Horse was not under attack, so he maintained a steady pace to prevent wearing out the ponies.

Another scout approached Gray Horse at a gallop and talked. Then he turned his pony and raced away towards the river.

"Let's go see what's going on," Hunt said to Earl and the Colonel.

"What is going on?" Hunt asked as he approached Gray Horse.

"A war chief by the name of Spotted Elk has crossed the river and has challenged Storm Warrior to a friendly match with no weapons. He claims he can defeat Storm Warrior and all will know his name as the man that has defeated Storm Warrior."

"Many Blackfeet chiefs have arrived at the river," Gray Horse continued, "and the Blackfeet numbers are close to five

175

thousand warriors. Spotted Elk says the warriors are anxious for battle, he thinks a friendly match could calm them; that is why he is challenging Storm Warrior."

"It could be a trick," Gray Wolf said, "they could get you to the bottom of the hill on the flat ground and attack across the river."

"Yes," Storm Warrior said, "but it would take them several minutes to cross the three foot deep water, by then I could climb the hill and escape."

"What if they have rifles and shoot you before you leave the flats," Gray Wolf asked?

"I do not think they would shoot with Spotted Elk there," Gray Horse said as he thought about the challenge.

Another scout rode in and reported that Red Elk and the Sioux warriors are only a mile away.

Numbering over forty-five hundred Sioux, made Gray Horse feel a little more comfortable.

"The Blackfeet will be at the river to watch the match," Gray Horse said. "We should also show up at the river to watch the match. The Blackfeet does not know how many Sioux they would be facing; I think having Red Elk's warriors and our warriors gather at the river and watch from the top of the hill will prevent an

176

attack. Our numbers will be much higher than they are thinking, and they will be glad they haven't attacked."

Gray Horse gave the order for all to mount up and then turned to talk to the Colonel and the Marshals.

"Storm Warrior has been challenged to a friendly match by a war chief by the name of Spotted Elk. The match will take place at the river. Red Elk and twenty-five hundred warriors are near; we will wait for them to join us.

"Beware," Gray Horse told them, "the Blackfeet may attack when Storm Warrior defeats their war chief. If the Blackfeet attack retreat to the canyon, shoot from behind the rocks."

Gray Horse, Storm Warrior and Gray Wolf rode out to meet Red Elk. Gray Horse quickly brought Red Elk up to date on what was happening.

As Gray Horse spoke Storm Warrior noticed Swimming Otter and a number of his students, four were red headbands, so he quickly developed a plan.

"Gray Horse," Storm Warrior said, "I have an idea to make this a little more interesting. There are four red headbands riding with Red Elk. Let us counter challenge Spotted Elk. He can choose four of his braves for a match with four of our young braves. Then after the four matches I will fight Spotted Elk."

177

"It could anger the Blackfeet if four of their best fighters and their war chief get defeated," Gray Wolf said.

"When the Blackfeet see our strength in numbers they will not attack," Storm Warrior said, "especially when they see how easily our young braves handle their warriors."

"We will see," Gray Horse said, "come we must go before the Blackfeet think we have decided not to accept Spotted Elk's challenge."

Storm Warrior asked Swimming Otter and the other red headbands to come with him.

Together Red Elk's warriors joined Gray Horse's warriors, and they rode to the top of the hill where Spotted Elk was waiting. Spotted Elk had begun insulting the Sioux scouts by saying it appeared that Storm Warrior was not going to come.

But his insults ceased when he saw the large number of Sioux coming towards him led by Gray Horse and Red Elk.

He noticed the warrior riding the magnificent black stallion with white hair flowing in the wind and knew this must be Storm Warrior.

The ridge of the hill stretched for nearly half a mile, the warriors spread out two deep and stopped at the top of the hill as they looked down and across the river at the Blackfeet that were gathered.

Chief White Hawk and the other Blackfeet chiefs looked across the river at the large number of Sioux. There were many more than they had expected.

Chief White Elk turned and looked at the other chiefs as he spoke. "It appears that Spotted Elk's scouts cannot count, it is good that we did not attack."

"Yes," the elder Chief Bull Bear muttered, "I wonder how many more Sioux are waiting out of sight."

Gray Horse approached Spotted Elk and stopped with Storm Warrior at his side as Hunt, Earl, and Lt. Colonel Hawks followed.

"What do you want?" Gray Horse asked?

"I have come to challenge your mighty Storm Warrior to a friendly match," Spotted Elk said as he glared at Storm Warrior.

"And what happens after the match is over?" Gray Horse asked.

Spotted Elk was a large and powerfully built warrior, nearly as large as Gray Wolf. He eyed the size and build of Storm Warrior and felt sure he could defeat him in a fair fight.

"After the match," Spotted Elk said confidently, "your warriors can come and retrieve the defeated Storm Warrior."

"I have four braves," Storm Warrior said, "that would like a chance to challenge four of your braves to a friendly match as well. After my four braves, defeat your four, we will complete our match. After the match, we will part friends and return to our camps."

"What four braves do you have that think they can defeat a Blackfoot warrior?" Spotted Elk asked.

Storm Warrior turned in his saddle and swept his arm to the four red headbands, "these four," Storm Warrior said.

Spotted Elk eyed the four braves sitting on their ponies and smiled.

"The Sioux," Spotted Elk said sarcastically, "think that these four young and inexperienced braves can defeat a Blackfoot warrior?"

"Yes," Storm Warrior said, "and after your four warriors are defeated I will defeat you."

"I will ride across the river and return with four braves," Spotted Elk said as he smiled. "We will meet you at the bottom of the hill where all can watch the Sioux be defeated."

"We will be there," Storm Warrior said.

Spotted Elk turned and rode his pony downhill and crossed the river. He joined the other chiefs and told them about the changes in the match.

Hunt, Earl and Lt. Colonel Hawks sat on their horses at the top of the hill next to Gray Wolf and Gray Horse as they watched Storm Warrior and five braves rode to the bottom of the hill and dismount.

One brave gathered the reins to the horses and stood off to one side while Storm Warrior and four braves wearing a red headband walked to the center of the grassy area and waited as Storm Warrior talked to the four young braves.

What's going on? Hunt asked Gray Wolf.

Spotted Elk had challenged Storm Warrior to a friendly match without weapons and Storm Warrior counter challenged him by offering to match four Blackfeet warriors against four of his red headbands. And after the four braves fight then Storm Warrior will fight

"This should be exciting," Earl said.

Hunt rolled a cigarette as he gazed down the hill and watched as five Blackfeet rode their horses across the river to join Storm Warrior and his four braves.

"Those Blackfeet look like bigger and older warriors," Hunt said, "I think the Blackfeet are trying to pull a fast one."

"Watch and learn," Lt. Colonel Hawks said as he looked at Hunt, "Storm Warrior has trained them."

Storm Warrior smiled, he knew that Spotted Elk would select four larger and stronger warriors, he knew it would only make his victory sweeter and would set the Blackfeet back on their ears to watch their larger and stronger warriors get defeated by the younger and smaller Sioux braves.

Hunt watched closely as Storm Warrior spoke to the group and a few moments later one of Storm Warrior's young braves and a larger Blackfoot warrior met in the center and began circling.

Hunt watched as the Blackfoot reached for the Sioux brave and the Sioux brave blocked his arms, kicked the Blackfoot in the ribs and then followed up with a kick to the back of the Blackfoot's head. The Blackfoot warrior went down hard and had a hard time standing.

Hunt and Earl watched as Storm Warrior approached the Blackfoot warrior and spoke to him. A few moments later Storm Warrior returned to the outer circle and the match resumed.

As the Blackfoot warrior approached the young Sioux kicked him firmly in the chest. The blow sent the Blackfoot sprawling backwards as he landed hard on his back.

"Looks like Storm Warrior is stopping the match," Earl said as they watched Storm Warrior helping the Blackfoot warrior to his feet and walked him over to where the Blackfeet were watching.

Hunt watched as the next Blackfoot warrior stepped into the center and flexed his muscles as he stretched and grinned at the young Sioux brave.

Hunt, Earl, and Lt. Colonel Hawks watched the next two matches. After three matches, Hunt couldn't believe that Storm Warrior's braves were defeating the Blackfeet warriors so easily.

'Watch this match," Lt. Colonel Hawks said to Hunt and Earl. "Swimming Otter is one of Storm Warrior's best students."

"I hope he's good," Hunt answered, "that Blackfoot looks like he wants to kill Storm Warrior," he said as they watched the Blackfoot approach Storm Warrior and spoke in an angry tone.

Hunt watched as the angry looking Blackfoot warrior attacked the young Sioux brave that the Colonel called Swimming Otter.

Moments later the Blackfoot was knocked to the ground and as he started to stand the Sioux brave kicked him hard in the side of the head causing the Blackfoot to roll several times.

After the Blackfoot stood he charged the Sioux brave and dived for his legs, but the Sioux spun and kicked him hard on the side of the head. This time the Blackfoot didn't get up.

Hunt watched as Storm Warrior stopped the young Sioux and approached the Blackfoot warrior.

"What do you think?" Lt. Colonel Hawks asked Hunt.

"I think Storm Warrior pulled one over on the Blackfeet," Hunt answered as he rolled another cigarette and watched Storm Warrior helping an injured Blackfoot warrior to his feet.

Then Hunt's attention was drawn to the arena as Storm Warrior and the Blackfoot chief known as Spotted Elk squared off in the arena.

Storm Warrior handled the larger Blackfoot easily. After the Blackfoot was knocked to the ground several times, kicked and flipped in the air, Storm Warrior and the Blackfoot appeared to be talking.

"Look," Earl shouted as he pointed, "a Blackfoot is going to shoot Storm Warrior."

Just then Swimming Otter called out, "look out Storm Warrior."

He turned to see the warrior, Angry Bull, standing by his pony with an arrow drawn back in his bow. Just as Storm Warrior turned the arrow was released.

Although the arrow was meant for Storm Warrior, Angry Bull's vision and coordination was off due to the kick to his head

184

by Swimming Otter during the match. Spotted Elk turned towards Angry Bull as the arrow was flying towards his chest. He was about to be killed by one of his own warriors.

Suddenly, Storm Warrior stepped in front of the frozen Spotted Elk and caught the arrow. Spotted Elk couldn't believe that Storm Warrior caught the arrow and saved his life. Immediately the other Blackfoot warriors grabbed the angry warrior's arms and held him.

Hunt watched as Storm Warrior and the Blackfoot talked and saw Storm Warrior hand the Blackfoot chief the arrow as the angry warrior that had shot the arrow struggled with the warriors holding him.

"What do you think of Storm Warrior?" Lt. Colonel Hawks asked as Hunt watched them collect their weapons, mount their ponies and start up the hill when the angry warrior turned and charged towards Storm Warrior with a knife drawn.

Spotted Elk turned his pony, and demanded the warrior to stop, but he kept going. Storm Warrior turned and saw Angry Bull charging with his pony at a full run with a knife in his hand. He intended to kill one or all of the Sioux in a suicide run.

Hunt drew his rifle and was about to shoot the Blackfoot when Storm Warrior attacked with his sabre drawn. Hunt decided to wait and see how this played out.

185

As their ponies drew near, Storm Warrior swiped the extended arm of Angry Bull holding the large knife.

Hunt, Earl and Lt. Colonel Hawks watched as Storm Warrior returned the saber to its sheath behind his back as the angry Blackfoot once again charged Storm Warrior.

Storm Warrior raised his leg and kicked Angry Bull firmly in the chest as he rode by. The kick sent Angry Bull spinning backwards off his pony landing hard on the ground. Storm Warrior stopped and sat on his horse and looked down at the injured Angry Bull just as Spotted Elk and the others rode up.

One of the warriors pointed towards the river and said something to Spotted Elk.

Hunt looked and to his surprise a Blackfoot chief with a large headdress of many feathers riding across the river alone.

Hunt couldn't hear what was being said as the chief that rode up was talking to the angry warrior, and then to Hunt's surprise the Blackfoot chief shot the angry warrior, talked to Storm Warrior and then turned and returned to the river as the other Blackfeet joined him.

"Now I've seen it all," Hunt said as he watched the Blackfeet leaving the river.

'Perhaps you may think so," the Colonel said, "but every time I'm around them I see something that totally amazes me."

Chapter 10

Shoshone Vengeance

Three days passed since the matches at the river and the dramatic ending to the matches with the Blackfeet.

The Sioux were at the Fort and were preparing to leave after safely delivering the Colonel and the U.S. Marshals.

Captain Blanchard reported that Charles Pollard and his two companions had left the previous day and were very angry at the way they had been treated and promised to file a formal complaint with Washington when they returned.

"I for one," the Colonel said, "am glad they're gone."

"Which way did they leave?" Hunt asked.

"They left the fort and traveled east," Captain Blanchard said.

"I don't think they will return in one piece," Hunt said as he lit his rolled cigarette.

"I think," the Colonel said to Hunt, "the chances of them making it past the Pawnee and the Shoshone is slim."

"Earl and I will leave tomorrow and head back to Denver to file my report," Hunt announced. "I want my superiors in Washington to receive my report prior to Charles Pollard returning and causing a big stink over nothing but his own agenda being foiled."

The next morning Hunt and Earl saddled their horses. They were about to leave when the sentry announced that Indians were approaching. "It looks like Storm Warrior and another chief," the sentry shouted down.

Lt. Colonel Hawks greeted them and invited them into the meeting room. Hunt and Earl joined them to hear what was going on.

After everyone was seated the Colonel asked, "what brings you to the fort today?"

"I have news of Judith's father," Storm Warrior said.

"Ok," Lt. Colonel Hawks said, "what is the news?"

"Judith's father and the other two white men are dead," Storm Warrior said.

188

"What happened to them?" The Colonel asked.

"It is said," Storm Warrior continued, "that the three-whites were traveling on the north side of the river to avoid the Shoshone and were spotted by the Pawnee. The Pawnee signaled for help and both Shoshone and Pawnee came. The Pawnee arrived first; there was shooting from the whites and the Pawnee returned fire."

"More Pawnee appeared and the whites crossed the river and lost their two-pack animals crossing the river. After crossing the river they were attacked by Shoshone, when the Shoshone attacked two Shoshone were killed," Storm Warrior said as he continued.

"An arrow hit one of the whites as they ran their ponies to the rocks for cover. They dismounted and climbed the hill and began returning fire. The Shoshone ran their ponies off and one of the Shoshone was injured while running off the ponies but will live," Storm Warrior added.

"More Shoshone arrived and they surrounded the hill and sent many warriors up the backside to attack from above. The white men were on foot, and they were surrounded. The Shoshone closed in at night and crept near to where the white men were hiding," Storm Warrior said as he continued.

"The Shoshone crept close enough to hear the whites talking, it is said that the whites were arguing and fighting among themselves, the injured man was crying in pain and the older man kept telling him to shut up or he would shoot him," Storm Warrior said.

"As the sun began to rise one of the whites came out with a rifle and a warrior shot him from above with an arrow, then the Shoshone rushed their position and the older man began firing a pistol but was also shot and was quickly taken captive along with the other two," Storm Warrior added.

"The Shoshone stripped them of their clothing and tied them behind ponies and drug them to a nearby hill covered by the large black ants," Storm Warrior said.

"They were tied down and then the fathers of the three-boys that were killed cut them open from their throats to their groin, then they castrated them and watched as the black ants covered their bodies."

"Pawnee were across the river several miles away and heard the screams of the three-white men for almost an hour and then they grew silent," Storm Warrior said. "The Shoshone left and returned to their camp, the boy's deaths had been avenged."

"Thank you for telling me about this," the Colonel said. "I'm sorry to say that I'm not sad about what happened to them."

"Can't say that I am either," Hunt added.

190

Chapter 11

Return To Denver

Hunt knew his job at the fort was finished. "I think it's time to head back to Denver," Hunt said to the Colonel after rolling a cigarette as he watched Storm Warrior and the other chief ride away to join the warriors waiting for them at the edge of the forest.

The Indians left the fort and headed west. "I was beginning to think you liked it here so much that you wanted to stay," Earl said with a smile.

"What did you think of riding with the Indians?" Hunt asked Earl.

"It's better than traveling with the soldiers," Earl answered. "They travel faster and have many more scouts."

"You know Hunt," Earl continued, "that day we were with the Sioux and we looked down across the river and saw five-thousand angry Blackfeet shouting war hoops I was very nervous. I looked around and the look on the Sioux chief's faces never changed, they just glared at them like they were daring them to attack."

"What did you think about the matches at the river?" Hunt asked.

"I think Storm Warrior was very smart, and it gave both sides a chance to blow off some steam and at the same time Storm Warrior showed compassion towards the Blackfeet by stopping matches before the warriors were seriously hurt," Earl answered.

"Yes," Hunt answered as he drew a puff on his cigarette, "had one of the Blackfeet been killed it would have given them an excuse to charge across the river and attack."

"OK," Hunt said to Earl, "let's go say goodbye to the Colonel and hit the trail."

Hunt and Earl spotted the army scouts Griz and Slim. "We're heading out," Hunt said as they shook hands.

"Say," Griz said with a grin. "I was in Denver a few years back. There's a saloon called Barnaby's and there was a healthy looking lady by the name of Dotty working there, just tell her Griz says hello."

"Oh hell," Slim cut in, "by healthy you mean fat."

"Yeah," Griz answered, "she had a little weight on her, but, she really knows how to treat a man."

Hunt and Earl chuckled. "OK," Hunt said, "if I ever get there I'll tell her."

"Thank you," Griz said with a smile.

The Colonel made sure Hunt and Earl had all the necessary food supplies when they left the fort.

Lt. Colonel Hawks and Captain Blanchard walked with Hunt and Earl to the front gate as they prepared to mount and ride out. Hunt and Earl shook both of their hands, then he thanked them for their hospitality, and then as the guard opened the gate they rode out.

It was noon when Hunt and Earl reached the campsite at the river crossing. They stopped to rest the horses and allow them to graze.

"The next hundred miles will be the most dangerous," Hunt said as he made notes in his journal.

It was late in the afternoon when they passed the place where they had met Bull on the trip to the fort. They carefully rode close to the eastern mountain range as they turned south and rode well past sundown and found a spot where they had camped on the journey to the fort.

193

The next day they continued on at dawn and were surprised that the site of the Cheyenne camp was vacant. They stopped to water the horses before continuing on. By nightfall, they had traveled more than sixty miles. Both horses walked briskly as Hunt and Earl kept a sharp eye on the landscape for trouble.

The remainder of the trip was uneventful. After many stops over the next three days in fledgling towns Hunt and Earl finally passed the tree where Hunt had made his mark.

Hunt stopped and looked at the tree. "Well Earl," Hunt said, "in a few hours, we'll be back in Denver and I've given our trip a lot of thought."

"What do you mean?" Earl asked as they rested the horses.

Hunt slowly rolled a cigarette and said, "About Storm Warrior, the two dead scouts, and the three men that the Shoshone killed. Unless someone was riding with us, they wouldn't believe our story. But I think we should report it as it really happened."

"You were starting to worry me," Earl said, "I planned all along to tell it the way it happened," he said with a smile.

"We've covered over four hundred miles over the past five days," Hunt said, "and it will be dark in a few hours. I don't know about you, but I'm ready for a steak & potato dinner, a nice cold mug of beer and a nice soft bed. So let's get on to Denver and finish our business."

194

Hunt and Earl continued on unaware that armed men were occupying Hunt's cabin.

They were small time criminals that robbed citizens at gunpoint and were planning to rob the Denver Stage before leaving the area and heading west for California.

They came across the cabin, and assumed it was an abandoned cabin. Even though Hunt had it stocked with canned vegetables and fruit. And they planned to kill whoever showed up to claim the cabin.

Chapter 12

Denver's First Judge Is Elected

Hunt and Earl made it to Denver by 6:00. Just as they rode into town they noticed U.S. Marshal Dodd coming from the office.

Dodd saw them coming so he stopped and greeted them.

"Well, well," Dodd said as Hunt and Earl stopped at the hitching post and dismounted, "I'm glad you made it back."

"We're glad to be back," Hunt said as he tied the reins to the hitching rail and shook hands. "I was just walking down to the café, would you like to join me?"

"Sure," Hunt said, "Earl and I both are craving for a big steak and potatoes. But first we have to take put our rifles away and take care of our horses."

Hunt and Earl carried their bedrolls, saddlebags and rifles inside and put them in the conference room then walked outside and walked their horses down to the livery.

"Give them a good rub down and an extra ration of oats," Hunt said to the livery stable hand, "they've been on a long ride and they're tired. First thing in the morning check their hooves and shoes."

"Sure will Marshal," the livery stable hand answered.

Hunt and Earl walked with U.S. Marshal Dodd to the café and settled at a corner table.

"I'm dying to know," Dodd said, "what did you find out about the missing scouts?"

"They're dead," Hunt answered. "With the help of some Sioux we found their bones, or at least what the coyotes didn't haul off, and buried them. I made a map of the location and marked their graves."

"What happened to them?" Dodd asked.

"I don't really know for sure," Hunt answered, "but next to one of the skulls we uncovered a Blackfoot arrow."

"So you think the Blackfeet killed them?" Dodd asked.

"I really don't know for sure," Hunt answered, "it could have been the Sioux. According to what I found out the Sioux were the last tribe they had visited before being killed."

"So they were on Sioux land?" Dodd asked.

"Yes, but they were found near the Blackfoot River, less than a mile away from Blackfoot land, and nearly six hours away from the Sioux camp."

"What's your gut feeling Hunt?" Dodd asked.

"We have three possibilities," Hunt answered as he cut into his steak. "According the Sioux, hunting and scouting parties from other tribes travel along the river going from one place to another. It's possible that one of these hunting parties had made camp in this box canyon where there's water, grass for the horses, and shelter. It could be that the three scouts rode into a hornet's nest."

"The second possibility is that the Sioux killed them," Hunt continued, "and the third possibility is that the Blackfeet killed them. If I had to lay wages on my choice I'd say the Sioux did it, but I can't prove it. The Sioux chiefs told me that the two scouts never told them that they were scouts; they told the Sioux they were traders."

'The white scouts wanted to know where the gold was, and when the Sioux told them there was no gold they became belligerent and the chief told them to leave and never come back," Hunt said.

"Did you meet the Sioux?" U.S. Marshal Dodd asked.

"Yes, Earl and I both spent the night in their camp," Hunt answered.

"That's interesting," Dodd answered, "tell me about them."

"Dodd," Hunt said as he looked at him, "if we operated our cities and government the same way the Sioux operate their camps we'd have a lot less crime."

"I got to know some of their chiefs, and I got a lot of insights from Lt. Colonel Hawks at the fort. They have a council that meets every night in a large lodge. Problems within the camp between people are openly discussed, and the chiefs resolve the issue and everyone lives with their decision. And when Chief Red Bear makes a decision it is final, no questions asked," Hunt answered.

"They have a number of war chiefs, but the head war chief goes by Gray Horse," Hunt said as he continued.

"Dodd," Hunt said as he looked at him, "if the U.S. Army had him for a General I'd feel sorry for any son-of-a-bitch that ever threatened the government. He's the smartest and craftiest leader I've ever seen."

"And then there's a chief by the name of Storm Warrior."

"I've heard the name before," U.S. Marshal Dodd said, "did you meet him?"

"I sure did," Hunt answered. "He runs a training camp for the young braves and teaches them how to fight. Earl will attest to this," Hunt continued, "we rode with five thousand Sioux and crested a hill that overlooked the Blackfoot River."

"On the other side of the river were close to five thousand Blackfeet yelling and screaming for war. There were three Sioux war chiefs, Gray Horse, Storm Warrior, and a Chief by the name of Gray Wolf, whom Storm Warrior claimed was a brother, but I doubt it," Hunt said.

"Why is that?" U.S. Marshal Dodd asked. "They look as different as night and day," Hunt answered."

"Gray Wolf is huge, he's over six foot four and weighs two hundred and forty pounds. He is dark skinned, black hair, and looks Indian. Storm Warrior is only about five foot ten, weighs a hundred and eighty five pounds, lighter skinned, white hair, and has green eyes. Even their voices are nothing alike. Gray Wolf speaks with a very deep grunting type of voice while Storm Warrior talks more like a college educated white man," Hunt answered.

"From what I was told," Hunt said, "Storm Warrior came to their camp a few years back and wanted to live with them. The tribal council decided that he would have to fight one of their warriors in a friendly match and if he won he could stay, if he lost he would have to leave. Chief Gray Wolf challenged him, and Chief Red Bear agreed."

"Then a chief by the name of Many Bears was Gray Wolf's father, he declared that if Storm Warrior won that Gray Wolf and Storm Warrior would become blood brothers," Hunt added.

"From what I was told the smaller Storm Warrior kicked Gray Wolf's ass and when it was over they became blood brothers and Many Bears accepted Storm Warrior as his son to replace the son that was killed the previous year in a battle with the Pawnee," Hunt said.

"I was told about a story that I didn't understand," Hunt said, "but when I left I did understand it."

"There was a conflict between the Blackfeet and the Sioux. Gray Wolf's horse fell on him trapping him under it. Five or six Blackfeet saw he was helpless and attacked when Storm Warrior rode through the battle to his rescue. He dismounted and stood between the Blackfeet and his helpless brother. Storm Warrior killed five or six Blackfeet that attacked with nothing but a knife. Then someone shot an arrow at Storm Warrior's heart and he caught the arrow, raised it over his head and broke it. After that, the Blackfeet turned and ran," Hunt said.

"He caught the arrow?" U.S. Marshal Dodd said as he chuckled, "That sounds more like a dime novel story than a real battle story."

"As God is my witness," Hunt said as he looked into U.S. Marshal Dodd's eyes, "I saw him do it at the river the day when the Blackfeet and the Sioux squared off across the river from each other."

"I saw it too," Earl added, "it was incredible."

"You mean there was a conflict?" Dodd asked.

"No, it turned out that one of the Blackfeet war chiefs by the name of Spotted Elk challenged Storm Warrior to a friendly match. From what I've heard all the tribes fear Storm Warrior and anybody that can defeat him will be a hero or something," Hunt said as he rolled a cigarette.

"Anyway," Hunt continued, "Storm Warrior had ideas of his own. He picked four young braves no more than fifteen or sixteen years old and told Spotted Elk to select four of his best fighters and to meet him down on the flats between the two war parties and they would fight a friendly match. So Spotted Elk rode back across the river and came back with four large warriors."

"You wouldn't believe it," Hunt said, "but Earl and I both watched Storm Warrior's four young braves kick the crap out of those four big Blackfeet. And then Storm Warrior had to fight Chief Spotted Elk."

"Spotted Elk was over six feet tall, and at least two-hundred pounds. Storm Warrior was beating him easily, and while Storm Warrior stopped to talk to him one of the indians that had been beaten by one of Storm Warriors kids grabbed a bow and shot an arrow."

"I think he was aiming for Storm Warrior, but he was pretty shook up after his beating and the arrow went straight for Spotted Elk's chest," Hunt said. "Storm Warrior jumped in front of him and caught the arrow. He saved Spotted Elks life."

"The Blackfeet mounted up and was heading back towards the river and the Sioux were headed back up the hill towards us when the Blackfoot that shot the arrow turned and attacked."

"Storm Warrior turned his horse and charged the Blackfoot with a sabre and knocked the knife from his hand, then Storm Warrior kicked him in the chest from horseback and knocked him off his horse," Hunt explained.

"Then a chief from the Blackfeet rode across the river and shot the warrior that had fired the arrow. It was the oddest thing I'd ever seen," Hunt said

"That sounds pretty incredible," U.S. Marshal Dodd said, "why do you suppose he shot his own man?"

"I was told," Hunt said as he sipped his coffee, "it was because he had dishonored the tribe. I'll tell you," Hunt said, "it sure as hell sent a message to the rest of them that when he says something he means it."

"These Indians," Hunt said, "everyone makes fun of them for being primitive but one thing they sure outshine us on and that's honor. When one of them is given an order it is done, no questions asked."

'Wow," U.S. Marshal Dodd said, "it sounds like you men had one hell of a trip, I can't wait to read your full report."

"We've been having some problems around here while you were gone," Dodd continued. "Settlers are moving in; a few have been robbed of their life savings. I have four men out trying to find them. They're working in pairs. Tomorrow I'd like you and Earl to set out and see what you can find."

"Gee," Hunt said, "after hanging that last bunch I thought folks would get the idea that we take that kind of thing serious around here."

"I think," U.S. Marshal Dodd said, "these are a couple of drifters just passing through, and I want them arrested before they kill someone or escape out of our area."

205

"So they haven't killed anyone yet?" Hunt asked.

"No, but they've scared the shit out of a few people," Dodd answered.

"I want these two," U.S. Marshal Dodd said with his eyes almost blazing, "it's a matter of time before they kill someone. Did you see anything suspicious as you came from the north?" He asked.

"No," Hunt answered, "we passed an old man on a wagon, he waved and we just kept riding."

"One of the families they robbed said they rode north. I sent Jason and Vance out; they rode about twenty miles and said they couldn't find anything.

"Did you have them check my cabin?" Hunt asked.

"No," Dodd answered, "they didn't."

"Well, Earl and I will turn in for the night at the hotel and head out there early tomorrow morning. With no one being around for the past two weeks it's possible that they found the cabin and are hiding out," Hunt said.

"I'll ride out with you in the morning," Dodd said, "Besides," he added, "I'd like to see this secret back entrance you're talking about in case I ever need to use it."

Early the next morning Hunt and Earl met U.S. Marshal Dodd at the café for breakfast.

"Vance and Jason rode in last night," U.S. Marshal Dodd said, "they had been searching south of Denver and didn't find anything. I told them we were going out this morning to your cabin and they want to ride along."

"I told them about some of your stories and they seem to think you're having all the fun," Dodd said.

"Yeah," Earl said, "they wouldn't think it was all fun if they slept out on the ground as many nights as we have over the past three weeks."

Then Jason and Vance walked in and joined them at the table.

"Well," Vance said, "while you two were on vacation we've been chasing ghosts all over the valley."

"Is that a fact?" Hunt asked. "Did you find your ghosts?"

"Nope, not a trace," Vance answered, "We scanned the entire area, except for a few isolated homes there was nothing. We talked to the people living in the cabins and those folks haven't seen any strangers. The only area not thoroughly searched so far is the north."

"The north is a large area," Hunt said as he sipped his coffee.

"Yes it is," Dodd answered, "and there are a lot of hidden valleys and mountains."

"We'll ride out and check your cabin Hunt, and it may be a good idea to use it as a base camp over the next few days as you four divide into two teams and scour the area," Dodd said.

"Unless," Hunt added, "we find the cabin occupied."

The five lawmen walked to the livery stable and the stable hand had just finished putting a fresh shoe on Hunt's horse's left front hoof.

"It was starting to come loose,' he said and it was unevenly worn so I just put a new one on. "He's ready to go."

"Thanks," Hunt said as he petted Walker's neck. They walked the horses outside, mounted and headed out of town.

Two hours later they came to the tree with the initials NW carved on it.

"Here's where we turn into the forest," Hunt said. "I marked this tree when Jed and I rode out to the road from the cabin. It's just a game trail part of the way but when we get closer I'll show you the landmark to look for."

208

Hunt led the way, and they followed in single file. After riding for about twenty minutes Hunt stopped and pointed to the twin peak visible through the trees.

"Watch for that peak," Hunt said as he pointed to the peaks, "The valley entrance is just below it."

Then he guided Walker through the trees and a short time later they came to the valley entrance.

Hunt stopped and held up his hand. "Remain quiet. The cabin will be visible right after we come out of the valley" he said in a soft voice.

They came out of the canyon and the roof of the cabin was visible over the treetops. They stopped and noticed a trickle of smoke coming from the chimney.

"OK," Hunt said, "someone is here, let's tie our horses here and circle the cabin. Earl," Hunt added, "work your way around to the barn, if they make a run for it they'll head straight for the horses."

Just as the lawmen got settled into position the front door opened and two men stepped out and started walking towards the corral.

Hunt had just walked up to the rear corner of the cabin when he heard the door close and men's voices. They were too close for the rifle, so he sat it down and drew his pistol as he stepped out.

"Stop and raise your hands," Hunt shouted.

Both men had their hands filled with saddlebags and bedrolls.

"Who the hell are you?" One of the men asked as they turned to face Hunt.

"I'm U.S. Deputy Marshal Porter," he answered, "and you men just walked out of my cabin on my property."

"So," one of the men said as he smiled, "this is your cabin is it?"

The man doing the talking tossed his bedroll and saddlebags down on the ground and the other man did the same.

"U.S. Deputy Marshal or not," he said, "I'm betting you're not good enough to take us both."

"He won't be alone," Earl said as he walked up behind them with his gun drawn.

Suddenly the other three Marshals appeared from behind the trees and around the front of the cabin with their rifles leveled.

"Drop the gun belts gentlemen," Hunt ordered.

The men looked around at the number of armed men that had them surrounded, the taller of the two that was doing the talking licked his lips nervously then shouted, "I'll be damned if I go to prison!" Then he went for his gun.

Hunt fired three shots in quick succession. The man was thrown backwards and landed flat on his back and didn't move. He died with his eyes wide open staring up at the sky.

"Either drop it or go for it!" Hunt shouted at the remaining man.

Slowly the other man reached down with a frightened look on his face and released the buckle allowing his gun to drop to the ground.

Hunt walked up behind him, and tied his hands behind his back, then searched him for more weapons. He found a small pistol and a knife under his coat and threw them onto the ground.

U.S. Marshal Dodd walked up and asked, "what's your name?"

"Logan," he answered nervously, "Josh Logan."

"And who was he?" Dodd asked.

"Brandon James," he answered as he looked down at his body.

"Brandon said he'd never be taken alive," Josh Logan said.

211

"Well, he kept his word," U.S. Marshal Dodd answered.

"Where's the money you two have been stealing from folks?" U.S. Marshal Dodd asked.

"In the saddlebags," Josh answered.

"It was Brandon that planned it," Josh said as Earl picked up the saddlebags.

"I don't care whose idea it was," U.S. Marshal Dodd answered, "you both robbed folks of their life savings and scared them half to death."

"Bring up our horses," Dodd said to Vance and Jason.

"Earl" Dodd said, "get those two horses saddled, we need to get back to Denver, Jed will be wondering where we're at."

"Mister," Josh said to Hunt, "I've seen Brandon draw and kill men when they had a gun on him, you sure surprised me by how fast you fired that Colt."

"He was foolish," Hunt said, "don't you give me any trouble on the way back or you'll see shooting him was no mistake."

"Brandon's got some kin," Josh said, "when they find out you killed him they'll come looking for you."

"That's fine," Hunt said, "I'll leave some grave sites vacant next to him so the family can be buried next to each other. Now mount up."

Josh Logan was helped up onto his horse's back and Brandon's body was tied over the back of his horse, and soon they were headed through the canyon and several hours later they stopped in front of the Sheriff's office where Josh Logan was locked up.

Bridge and Jason took the body of Brandon James to the back door of the morgue and dropped his body off.

U.S. Marshal Dodd walked to the telegraph office and wired Chicago asking for any information on Brandon James and Josh Logan while Hunt and Earl walked the horses to the stables.

Minutes later they all met at the café for a well-deserved meal and were joined by Sheriff Collins. They occupied a long table at the back of the room.

"I'm glad we found those two," U.S. Marshal Dodd said, "job well done men."

"Next time," Jed said angrily, "wait for me." Everyone chuckled at that.

"Bridge tells me," Jed continued, "when you shot that guy that you could cover all three bullet holes with a silver dollar."

"Well," Hunt answered, "with only six feet between us I think anyone at this table could do that."

"Yeah," Bridge said, "but you fired all three shots so fast that it sounded like one shot."

"Well," Hunt said as he lifted his coffee cup, "let's just say I was scared." This made everyone laugh.

"I'm glad it turned out well for you men," Sheriff Collins said, "and no one got hurt."

"If it was me and my men I'm afraid someone may have frozen and gotten killed," Sheriff Collins said.

"Your men are all young," U.S. Marshal Dodd said, "give them a little time and a little practice."

"That's easy for you to say," Sheriff Collins said as he smiled, "you stole my best man."

"Now, now," Dodd answered as he smiled, "he was my man all along; I just loaned him to you for a few days."

"I assume you're talking about Clayton," Hunt said, "how is he doing?"

"I sent him to Chicago last week," Dodd answered, "he has to go through the academy."

Then Dodd laughed, "I received a wire from Marshal Bekins, all it said was, where the hell did you find him?" Once again, everyone laughed.

"Apparently he has been telling the instructor what he's doing wrong and wants to argue about everything," Dodd said.

"I received a 2nd wire from Bekins and he said Clayton aced the shooting class," Dodd added.

"That sounds like Clayton all right," Hunt said with a chuckle.

"Yes, it sure does," Sheriff Collins said with a laugh. "He thinks my deputies were so young that, he even asked me if I have to allow the deputies time off for school."

"Actually," Sheriff Collins said, "he took a few of my deputies out and target practiced with them. It turned out that they liked him, and all of them agreed they were better shots after he showed them a few tricks."

"That's sound," Dodd said, "everyone needs a little time to get experience at their work and mature a little."

"Yes," Sheriff Collins said, "now I just need to work on their bravery points a little."

"When will the circuit judge be coming through?" Hunt asked.

"Actually," Sheriff Collins said, "Denver has its own judge now. Last month the city council met and with the way the town is growing the addition of two more deputies was approved, as well as electing a judge. The committee felt that with the load of legal cases constantly growing we needed our own full time judge."

"So we looked at all the attorneys and one man stood out. Franklin Straw was an attorney and had worked as a judge in New York for a short time before moving to Denver. He's older; level headed and really knows the law. He didn't have a lot of clients due to what he charged for attorney fees, but being semi-retired he really didn't care. The town council approached him, and he accepted. He said he was about to close his law office, and the thought of being the first judge in Denver appealed to him," Sheriff Collins said.

"Judge Straw is a little strange," Sheriff Collins said, "he wanted more money but settled on what the city was willing to pay providing the city did something for him to stroke his ego."

"What did he con the city council into doing for him?" Earl asked.

"He said that if they put a painting of him in the courthouse with the title of "Denver's First Judge" to be left there forever, even after his death as a memorial, he would accept the job with the pay they offered. The city agreed. It speaks of his ego; he really

216

didn't need the money; he is fairly wealthy and at his age he's more concerned with being important and being remembered."

"How old is he?" Hunt asked.

"He's sixty-two," Sheriff Collins answered.

"Well," U.S. Marshal Dodd said, "it looks like Josh Logan will be his first high profile case."

"Judging by Judge Straw's ego I'd say he would like to make an example of how tough he plans to be, by hanging the son-of-a-bitch and setting an example for other thieves and lawbreakers," Sheriff Collins added.

"I hope you're right," U.S. Marshal Dodd answered, "and the city of Denver's law needs to have some teeth. Criminals, crooks, thieves and convicts need to know that Denver won't put up with their crap, and we got the lawmen here and the court system to handle them."

The men all left the café and headed home. Earl was walking next to Hunt.

"How would you like a cold beer," Earl asked.

"Sounds good to me," Hunt answered.

They stopped off at the saloon and entered. Heads turned when they walked in and the laughter died down a little.

Hunt and Earl sat at the bar and ordered a beer.

"I'm glad you're here," the bartender said in a low voice. "The man down the bar, with the buckskins is getting drunk and obnoxious."

"Tell him he's done," Hunt said, "and send him home. If he gets out of line, I'll handle it."

A short time later the man in buckskins slammed his mug on the bar so hard that it broke.

"Bartender," he shouted, "I want another beer, why the hell are you so slow?"

"You've had enough," the bartender said in a loud voice; "it's time for you to go sleep it off."

"What!" The belligerent drunk said as he pulled out a large knife, "how would you like me to skin your head?"

Hunt quickly walked up to the man and grabbed his wrist holding the knife, the other hand held a pistol to the man's head.

"The bartender said you've had enough, and I agree, it's time for you to go home or I'll have to lock you up," Hunt said in a firm tone as he glared at the man.

"Who the hell are you?" He asked in an angry voice.

"I'm U.S. Marshal Porter, and this is U.S. Marshal Jefferson, we will either shoot you on the spot or you can go home and sleep it off, what will it be?" Hunt asked.

"You don't know who the hell I am, do you," the man said with a snarled lip.

"Yes I do,' Hunt answered, "you're a belligerent drunk and I agree with the bartender, you've had enough."

"OK," the man said, "you've got the drop on me so I'll leave."

Hunt released the grip on his wrist and backed off while keeping his pistol held ready.

The man in buckskins grinned as he put his knife back into its sheath. "Partner," he says, "I just got to Denver after being out on the prairie for a spell, hell, I'm just having a little fun and trying to unwind."

"That's fine," Hunt said, "but this ain't the prairie; this, is Denver and people here show a little respect for others."

"The name's Buck Dawson," the drunken man slurred. "I just got back from the Indian Territory up north, and there ain't much to drink up there."

"Yes I know," Hunt answered. "Now let's get going, you got a place to stay?"

219

"Not yet, but hell that ain't nothing new, I can sleep on the ground or in the stables, I don't care," Buck answered.

"Well, the man that owns the stables might care," Hunt answered. "I want you to get a hotel room or leave town."

"Yeah? Well, I'll go check out the hotel and see if they have a room, I haven't slept in a bed in more than two months," Buck said as he staggered a little.

"OK, Mr. Buck Dawson," Hunt said, "I'll be checking with the hotel to make sure you checked in. If you haven't you'd better hope I don't see you in town, and if I do see you in town you had better be sober and not causing any problems."

"OK Marshal," Buck said as he chuckled, "you folks sure know how to go out of your way to make a feller feel welcome."

Buck bent over and picked up a large pack and grabbed a rifle by its barrel and headed out with his backpack hitting a lady in the shoulder on his way out.

"Thanks Hunt," the bartender said, "I had a feeling he was going to get ugly; I'm glad you fellers were here."

"That's all right," Hunt said, "we'll have two more beers then we'll be on our way."

"Coming right up," The bartender said with a smile.

Just as Hunt, and Earl were about to drink their beer an older well-dressed gentleman with white hair and a white mustache walked up to them and stopped.

"I overheard you say you were U.S. Marshals," the man said.

"That's right," Hunt answered, "I'm U.S. Deputy Marshal Huntley Porter, and this is U.S. Deputy Marshal Earl Jefferson.

"Pleased to meet you," the man said as he extended his hand, "I'm Judge Franklin Straw."

"Oh yes," Earl said as they shook hands, "you are Denver's newest Judge."

"I'm the first Judge of Denver," he said as his eyes narrowed.

"I stand corrected," Earl said as he smiled.

"I just wanted to compliment you on the way you handled the drunk, I was enjoying a drink with a business associate and we couldn't help but notice the gentleman was getting out of line," Judge Straw explained.

"The problem with some of the men that have been out on the prairie for months and come to town is that they want to have a good time. And most of the time their idea of having fun is very annoying to others. I don't really think he meant any harm; he was just letting off some steam," Hunt answered.

"I understand," Judge Straw said, "the U.S. Marshals arrested a man accused of robbery and another man was killed during the arrest."

"Yes, that's right," Hunt answered.

"I'll let it be known," Judge Straw said, "I won't condone using excessive force when making an arrest, I think perhaps, the man could have been taken into custody to stand trial if professionalism and proper protocol had been exercised," he said with a scowl on his face.

"Well Judge," Hunt said, "we did exercise professionalism and proper protocol, the man was surrounded by five armed U.S. Marshals, we announced who we were, and he was told to raise his hands. But what would you have done if the man screamed that he wasn't going to jail and drew his weapon? Would you just stand there and let him shoot you and the other U.S. Marshals, or would you have the sense to shoot him first?"

"If that's the way it happened, the man or men responsible would not have to face retribution," Judge Straw said, "but the incident will be investigated, wearing a badge is not a license to kill."

"You're talking to the man that shot him Judge," Hunt said as his eyes narrowed, "and what I just told you is the way it happened."

"He's right," Earl said as he spoke up, "I was there and that is the way it happened."

'Well then," Judge Straw said as he placed his hat on his head, "after reviewing the written statements from the others you won't have anything to worry about. Good evening gentlemen," he said as he turned and walked away.

"He sure sounds like an arrogant son-of-a-bitch," Earl said after the Judge left.

"Yeah," Hunt answered, "I just hope he's as tough on the ones we arrest."

"We'll find out," Earl said.

"We need to talk to the families that were robbed," Hunt said, "we need one or more that can identify him as one of the robbers."

The next morning at the U.S. Marshal office everyone gathered in the conference room as U.S. Marshal Dodd addressed them.

"Gentlemen," Dodd said, "on the wall is a map of the western area that we are expected to cover. For the time being, I've

223

drawn lines dividing the territory into six parcels. Each of you is assigned a parcel and is responsible for that parcel."

"If at any time you need help you are to return to this office, explain to me what's going on and if it sounds like all you need is one more man I'll go with you. If the problem involves more support we'll call on the men from other territories and we'll all go out together. Under no circumstance are you to put yourself into a situation where you are outnumbered or the chances of getting killed are high," Dodd said.

"Now, for more immediate concerns," Dodd added, "Judge Straw has issued a court order to look into the death of the man that was killed yesterday during the arrest. Only Jed is excluded, everyone else, including me, are required to write out exactly what happened and what led up to the shooting. No one is to speak to any other; you are to write what you saw and heard, and nothing else, and you are not to discuss it with each other. And I want it done now while the events are still fresh in everyone's mind, any questions?"

Jed got up, and left while the others wrote out the events leading up to the killing of the suspected robber, and handed them to U.S. Marshal Dodd.

Chapter 13

DENVER'S FIRST JUDGE MAKES HIS MARK

Two days passed since U.S. Marshal Dodd turned the written statements into the Judge's office and a trial was arranged for Josh Logan.

Two families were located in Denver that had been victims of the robbery and were present in the courtroom when Sheriff Collins and four of his deputies brought in Josh Logan through the back door.

Judge Straw entered and everyone stood. After he was seated everyone else sat and the court officer announced the trial of one Josh Logan accused of armed robbery was in session.

The U.S. Marshals were seated in the front row behind the defendant and the lawyers took turns making their opening statements to the jury. One by one the victims were asked to take the stand and describe what happened then asked if they could identify the accused as one of the robbers. Three said yes and pointed to Josh Logan, one woman claimed, she wasn't sure, but said he looked like one of the men.

The prosecutors then called, U.S. Marshal Dodd and U.S. Deputy Marshal Porter to the stand to testify. Both told what had happened and both were harshly cross examined by the defense attorney. However, they never varied from their story.

The defense attorney accused Hunt of murdering one of the suspects when the Judge spoke up and cautioned him to avoid accusing anyone of anything except for the accused.

Hunt stuck to his story, "the suspect was going for his gun and I shot him," Hunt answered.

U.S. Marshal Dodd backed up his story by saying, "the man had cleared his holster before Hunt fired the first shot."

Finally the jury retired to decide on the fate of Josh Logan. It was late afternoon when the jury announced they had reached a unanimous decision. The courtroom was filled when the head juror stood and announced that the jury has found the defendant guilty of multiple armed robberies.

Judge Straw gazed at the courtroom and said, "The Denver area is attracting a lot of people from all parts of the United States and I hope one day Denver will be a significant city. We the people of Denver have no passion in our heart for those that prey on folks moving into our territory to start a new life. Today its robbery and tomorrow it could be murder."

"I want the people of Denver to know that we will not condone criminal activity," Judge Straw said as he continued, "especially those preying on hard working families and others moving into the city. The court sentences you to hang by the neck until dead at noon tomorrow, court, is adjourned," he said as he slammed his gavel on his desk and left the courtroom.

The court officer approached U.S. Marshal Dodd and Hunt and said the judge wanted to see them in his chambers.

U.S. Marshal Dodd and Hunt entered the Judge's Chambers.

After the door was shut the judge looked at them and said, "I've read the written testimonies, and you're in the clear this time. But next time make sure they appear in my court."

"I want the people of Denver to know that I won't condone thievery, murder or robbery. When you shoot, and kill a suspect you are robbing the victims of justice. In the future, I want criminals brought before me, understand?" Judge Straw asked as his eyes narrowed.

"Yes your honor," U.S. Marshal Dodd answered. "We will deliver every criminal that we can before you, but I won't allow my Marshals to place themselves in harm's way to bring the killer to your court if it could cost them their life."

"Very well," Judge Straw answered, "just make sure your Marshals give the suspects a fair opportunity to surrender without being gunned down," he said as he looked at Hunt.

"I will do that Your Honor," U.S. Marshal Dodd said.

"Very well," Judge Straw said, "just make sure your Marshals know they are not to act as judge, juror, and executioner, understand?"

"Yes, we understand," U.S. Marshal Dodd answered.

"Very well," Judge Straw said. "By the way, after reviewing the reports written by you and your U.S. Marshals I find no fault in U.S. Marshal Porter's actions. But next time," Judge Straw said as he glared at Hunt, "try to wound them, let me execute them."

"I will do what I can," Hunt answered.

The next day the city was buzzing with people flocking into town to see the hanging. U.S. Marshal Dodd and his five marshals, Sheriff Collins and his four deputies comprised the total law enforcement to contain the crowd of over fifteen hundred people.

Josh Logan was brought out, and the crowd parted to allow the Sheriff and his deputy's room to be escorted to the gallows.

"Hang you son-of-a-bitch," an older man that had been a victim of Josh Logan and his partner.

A few minutes later Josh Logan was standing on the gallows floor, and a rope was placed around his neck and a hood placed over his head. A preacher said a prayer and minutes later the hangman pulled the lever and Josh Logan died.

Judge Straw watched the hanging from his office window. Josh Logan was the first man he sentenced to hang, and in the future, he knew there would be more. Judge Straw watched as the men lowered Josh Logan's body onto a wagon and then he watched as the crowd dispersed.

He noticed U.S. Marshal Porter looking up at him standing in front of the window and watched as Hunt turned and walked away.

Judge Straw knew he was a good lawman, and he knew that in the future he would be disciplining other lawmen for killing a suspect, but for some reason he had a sincere interest in U.S. Marshal Porter.

His eyes are too cold, Judge Straw thought, there's something sinister about that man.

COMING SOON

HUNT-U.S. MARSHAL IV

The Hunt-U.S. Marshal series continues with serious drama as Hunt leads the U.S. Deputy Marshals on a long journey to bring cattle thieves to justice; however it ends in a dramatic gun battle.

A well-organized gang of Mexican bandits are terrorizing the west as they round up cattle and head them to Mexico to feed an army of men determined to overthrow the Mexican government.

It will be up to the U.S. Marshals to stop this intrusive army of predators and bring them to justice. With an army of several hundred men the Mexicans decide to strike Denver and free their leaders that were arrested and being held in the Denver jail.

This time it may be too much for the U.S. Marshals to handle by themselves, forcing them to wire the closest Army post for help.

The next book includes gun battles, deadly moonshiner problems, falling in love with a beautiful widow, discovering gold, starting a cattle herd, a wedding and an army of angry Mexicans threatening to kill everyone in Denver and burning the town to the ground.

DON'T MISS THE ADVENTURE

OTHER BOOKS WRITTEN BY

WL COX

STORM WARRIOR

STORM WARRIOR II

STORM WARRIOR III

HUNT-U.S. MARSHAL

HUNT-U.S. MARSHAL II

Made in the USA
Monee, IL
11 June 2021